Once upon a time in Harlem

a novel written by:

Moses Miller

This novel is a work of fiction. Any resemblances to real people, living or dead, actual events, establishments, organizations, locales are intended to give the fiction a sense of reality and authenticity. Other names, characters, places and incidents are either products of the author's imagination or are used fictitiously.

Once Upon a Time in Harlem is a work of
F.E.D.S. Fiction
Published by:
Clark, Inc.
1324 Lexington Avenue
Suite 340
New York, NY 10128

Copyright 2007
ISBN 10: 0-9797031-0-7
ISBN 13: 978-0-9797031-0-2

Written by Moses Miller, courtesy of Mind Candy, LLC.
Edited by C.P.I., Inc.
Cover design by Marion Designs

Printed in the United States

Antoine Clark would like to thank his children: Keonda Clark, Alayah Clark and Chazz Clark. And also his nephews Jamel and Jayden Clark.

*The history of **Harlem** can be described as a rise and fall, or an ever-changing journey with interesting twists and turns that help formulate many intriguing tales. Once occupied solely by Native Americans, and then the Dutch and British, this place once called "Nieuw Haarlem", is rich in culture and identity.*

The name originated from the Dutch when they settled here in the 1650's. It was named after one of their towns in the Netherlands. The Dutch farmers used Black slaves to farm their land, and to also help build roads. Sometime in the 1830's, the railroad that would eventually become known as the Metro North was built through **Harlem**, which helped transform this beautiful land into a wealthy city within a city.

*In the early 1900's, more African Americans from the south began to migrate north in droves, looking for new opportunities for a better life and increased income. Several of these "country folk" ended up settling in **Harlem**, NYC.*

Phillip Payton, a Black businessman and realtor, acquired several properties previously owned by whites, and made them readily available to middle class Black folk. Thus, these neighborhoods became filled with Blacks from the West Indies and the south. Areas such as "Sugar Hill" (145th to 155th street), "Strivers Row" (West 138th and 139th street) and Graham Court (116th and 117th street) became populated with affluent Blacks ranging from lawyers, doctors, artists and musicians.

*The customs and art forms that would emerge from this influx of people, would be unlike anything ever experienced in the north. **Harlem** would eventually become known as the Mecca for creative literature, jazz music and other fine arts.*

Harlem was the home to such prominent figures as Thurgood Marshall, W.E.B Dubois, Walter White and Roy Wilkins. It would also be the key area of operations for organized criminals such as Madame St. Clair, Bumpy Johnson, Red Dillon, Frank Lucas, Nicky Barnes, Frank Matthews, New York Freddie Myers, Pee Wee Kirkland, Preacher, Fritz, Rich Porter, Alpo, etc, etc, etc…

With the help of the mafia, the government and other forces, the beautiful landscape once considered the land of opportunity for Blacks, would be transformed into a haven for the numbers racket, heroin, cocaine and eventually crack distribution.

ONCE UPON A TIME IN HARLEM

Once
upon a time
in
Harlem

a novel written by:

Moses
Miller

Consumption

CHAPTER 1

It was approximately 8 o'clock on a Saturday night, and 138th street was uncharacteristically silent and dark. This was the area of Harlem known as "Striver's Row", because of the fancy brownstones that had been built in the 1920's, which became occupied by the black upper class. Even after forty years had passed, the buildings still looked physically appealing, even though the tenants had changed.

The sun had set, and the only illumination came from the streetlights that lit up the hard pavement. Long gone were the people and the hustle and bustle that existed only hours before. Those that remained scattering about, were just hanging out jive talking or making plans for the evening. The ladies were home digging through their closets, trying to scrap together their best digs to wear over to Mr. B's, Woody's, Shalimar or Big Wilt's club. They knew that the hustlers and gamblers would be out in force tonight, and only the finest freaks would have a shot at catching their eye and spending their cash.

John Williams sat slouched down behind the steering wheel of his rusty old blue 57' Chevy Impala. He was draped in a raggedy pair of blue overalls, and a dingy white t-shirt that had oil and dirt smeared on it from a hard day's work. Although he looked older, John was only twenty-three years old. Years of working as a mechanic and a handyman, had left him with a face sculpted with hardened features and a chiseled frame. He took the painstaking trip up from the south with his 17 year-old brother Sam earlier in the year, in search of opportunities in the big city. At that time, he confidently told his girlfriend Michelle that he would send for her as soon as he got things situated. He was always good with his hands, and was certain that he wouldn't have any problems finding work and decent pay.

The opportunity well had run dry in South Carolina, and John and Sam found themselves doing petty robberies and muggings in order to provide money to put food on the table. In the big apple, he wouldn't have to sit incognito outside of a juke joint, waiting for an unsuspecting patron to leave drunk at the end of the night, so he could pounce on them. Those days were over...so he thought. Six months passed like the blink of an eye, and John was still broke and struggling to find work to help ends meet. He began to realize that the racism that was prevalent in the South, existed in a more subversive fashion in the North. At least the bigots he encountered in South Carolina called him "nigger" to his face. Up here they plotted against you behind your back, while they smiled in your face.

When he lived down south, the good ole' southern cooking helped keep his 5-11' frame thick at a healthy 215 pounds. Lately, the lack of money and infrequency of meals, had visibly taken its toll, causing his physique to slowly decay. As his sweaty palms gripped the steering wheel, John stared at himself in the rear view mirror. He looked beyond the hairy stubble forming on his face, shocked to see how thin and drawn in his once round face had become. After studying himself for a couple of minutes, he gazed back at the streets, regaining his composure and concentration. He didn't have time to think about anything else but what he came here for tonight. He tried to do the right thing and live by the straight and narrow, but he felt himself being forced back into a life of crime.

A light drizzle began to fall from the sky, glazing the ground with a light coat of rain, and increasing the humidity significantly. Those that were still on the street scattered in sight of the summer rain, as if they thought a little water would make them melt.

"I'm hungry as hell," Sam said. He was always at John's side as far back as he could remember. Racist Klan's men gruesomely murdered their father when they were still in grade school, and their mother had succumbed to the pains of cancer just last year. Since then, John had been doing his best to provide for himself and his little brother.

Sam looked like a younger version of John, except he was slightly thinner and his complexion was a shade lighter. Even though he was only seventeen, his young eyes had seen a lot in his short life, and he was wise beyond his years. The two of them were so close that they sometimes finished each other's sentences for one another. And they always seemed to know what the other one was thinking. Sam sat in the passenger's seat keeled over holding his stomach, with his head resting on the dashboard.

"Just be patient, we'll get some food in a little while," John said assuredly.

Exasperated, Sam glared at John in disgust. "You said that an hour ago. Man, I'm fuckin' starving," he said while moaning loudly to add more emphasis. John glanced over at him. He did look like he was in a great degree of agony. John was just about to reach into his pocket and give him a half eaten *Mary Jane* bar, when he noticed a break in the darkness in his peripheral vision.

It was Hayward Jones, the local numbers runner who was making a little money for himself, judging by his tailor made silk and suede wears. Hayward was a flamboyant character who liked being noticed, and was always looking for attention. Even though no one was out on the block, he bopped slowly across the street, as if he was walking down a red carpet to a movie premiere. John had been following his routine closely for the past week, studying his every move carefully. He was right on time as usual.

"Here," John said throwing the candy bar over to Sam. "I'll be right back."

As soon as the candy bar hit the seat, Sam snatched it up like a starving hostage and took a healthy bite out of it.

"Where you going?"

"I got some business to take care off."

"I'm coming too," Sam said adamantly. He was used to going everywhere with John.

"No, stay here," John responded sternly. "Sit behind the wheel n' start the car when you see me come out the door." That was all he needed to hear to be content. He didn't have a driver's license, so he cherished every opportunity his brother gave him to drive.

"O.K." Sam said, cracking a wide grin.

"Remember. Pump it twice before you turn the key, and don't over pump—" John started to remind him, before being interrupted.

"I know, I know."

The darkness of the night enveloped John, as he walked briskly but quietly across the wet pavement. He was trying to blend in discreetly, but his raggedy clothes made him stick out like a sore thumb. Hayward had just entered the building. John waited patiently, before pushing the door open behind him slowly and entering the vestibule.

After completing a handyman job earlier that day for the tenant downstairs, he had rigged the door jam by placing a wad of gum in it, so the lock didn't fully engage when you closed the door. John knew that Hayward's apartment was on the second floor, because he had followed him here before. He quickly removed his dirty work shoes and left them at the bottom of the stairwell, before creeping up the rickety old staircase that led to the second floor.

The stairs made a slight creaking noise under the pressure of his body weight, but not enough to alarm anyone. Hayward had just unlocked his door and was about to enter his apartment when John reached the top of the steps.

"Yo, Hey," he yelled out. His tone was just loud enough to get him to turn around, but not so loud that it would garner the attention of his neighbors.

"Who dat," Hayward asked, as he put his right hand on his brow and peered down the poorly lit hallway.

"It's me," John said as he continued to walk towards his direction. Once he got closer, Hayward cracked a sinister smile as he recognized who it was.

"Country? What the hell is your old simple ass doing in my building boy?" He asked sarcastically.

"I'm still looking for work. Do you have any thing for me yet?"

"Look at you nigga. Yo, dumb ass so po that you ain't even got no shoes on your feet. Shiittt...Simple ass nigga. Last time I seen you, didn't I tell you not to ask me for work no more, nigga?" Hayward said agitatedly as he glared at John. His muscular frame began to tighten up as he became more upset.

"Actually, you said next time I ask you for some work, you was gon' kill me," John said, as his voice cracked out of nervousness. His southern drawl was more pronounced now, as it always was when he was upset or agitated.

"So, what the fuck is you doing here, you dumb motherfucker?"

"Well, I asked for work...and I ain't dead yet," John said sarcastically, as he glanced directly into Hayward's eyes with a slight smirk on his face. His blood felt like it was beginning to boil due to the adrenaline rushing throughout his body. He gathered his thoughts, and continued talking. "So, not only is your word worth shit, but you ain't got a lick of balls on ya' either."

Hayward shot a menacing glare at John, as he angrily yelled out "Motherfuc —"

Before he could finish his sentence, John swiftly pulled a sharp sharecropper's knife out of the back pocket of his overalls. Hayward's eyes widened, but he was completely caught off guard as John sliced his throat in one motion, violently ripping through the muscles that lined his neck.

Blood shot out splattering the white hallway wall, and spraying John in the face.

Instinctively, Hayward lunged forward forcefully grabbing John around the throat with both of his pudgy hands. John tried to maintain his stance, but his socked feet couldn't gain any traction on the slippery polyurethane floor. Hayward easily used his upper body strength to plow him backwards, slamming him into the wall. As he banged into the hard plaster, the knife jarred loose from John's hand, and slid across the floor.

A steady flow of thick blood ran out of Hayward's neck, drenching the front of his white silk shirt in a deep red color. John struggled valiantly, trying to pry his hands from his neck, but to no avail. His mouth fell open as he gasped for air, while the grip continued to grow increasingly tighter around his neck. It was as if the loss of blood was making Hayward stronger instead of weakening him.

"Ughhh...Ha....mug...Uh," Hayward spewed out inaudibly, struggling to put together a sentence. Blood seemed to stain every one of his exposed teeth, as he cracked a smile and continued to flex his muscles, effectively putting more pressure on John's neck. The sarcastic grin on his face made it obvious that he was trying to taunt him, but the wound to his neck was causing the words to come out as incomprehensible gibberish. John tried to muster as much strength as he could to knee him in the groin, but Hayward's massive body was pressed too tightly against his frame for him to gain any type of leverage. As he started to feel lightheaded, he made a mental note. No matter what happened, he would never underestimate a foe again...if only he survived this ordeal.

Hayward's smile widened, realizing that John's body was growing limp, and his defenses were weakening. Bloody drool ran down his chin in a steady stream, as he continued to crack his menacing smile. His eyes were locked in a dead stare with John, as the precious seconds that passed seemed like an eternity. Veins were visible in Hayward's forehead as he strained. He continued to flex his muscles, putting all of the strength he could muster into his wrists.

"Uhhhhhh!" Hayward yelled out in extreme agony, as he spit a mouth full of thick blood and saliva into John's face. His grip loosened, as his body went limp and crumpled to the floor with a loud thud. John put his hands to his neck and coughed a few times as he struggled to get oxygen and breathe normally. After gaining his composure, he wiped his face and looked downward at Hayward's limp body, noticing that his sharecropper's knife was protruding out of his back. When he looked back up, he saw his little brother Sam standing there.

Sam was stone faced, and there was a slight glint of madness in his cold eyes. John walked over to him and gave him a tight hug. He couldn't remember ever being so happy to see his little brother's face. He had intentionally told Sam to stay in the car because he didn't want things to escalate. He knew that Sam had a bad temper, and tried his best to keep him away from testy situations. Ironically, Sam had just saved his life.

"Thanks, Sam. That motherfucker there was strong as shit," John said.

"I told you to let me come inside with you," Sam said, as he cracked a sarcastic smile before continuing. "Man, that motherfucker almost killed your skinny ass."

"Nah, I was just about to put a whooping on his ass, before you came and ruined my plan."

"Yeah right. Why didn't you tell me that you was coming in here to kill that nigga?"

"Cuz I didn't plan on killing him...you killed him, motherfucker," John said, with a slight grin on his face before continuing. "But, seriously. He was asking for that shit. He was talking to me like his bitch. What made you come up here any way?"

"You was up here so long, I thought you was eating dinner or some shit. I told you I was starving," Sam said laughing before continuing. "Are we gonna—" John interrupted him by putting the pointer finger on his left hand to his mouth and saying, "Shhh."

He thought he heard a noise emanating from the staircase, so he focused his attention down the hallway, but didn't notice anyone. The events that just transpired had caused quite a ruckus, and he wanted to make sure none of the neighbors nosily wandered upstairs.

Satisfied that the coast was clear, he looked at Sam and said, "Help me drag this heavy motherfucker into the apartment."

Sam bent over and ripped the bloody knife out of Hayward's spine, wiping the thick red blood on his expensive silk shirt before placing it in his own back pocket. He grabbed Hayward's limp body by the ankles, struggling to hoist up his 250-pound frame, as John grabbed his arms around the wrists. As they picked him up, blood seeped out of his back steadily flowing onto the shiny wood floor. They carried him into the living room of his apartment and quietly dropped him down on an Oriental rug that adorned the beautifully decorated room. John huffed and puffed, still struggling to get his breathing right, as he walked over and locked the apartment door behind them. Without hesitation, Sam removed Hayward's expensive gold jewelry from his neck and wrists, and began sifting through the pockets on his suede pants like a scavenger.

"Jackpot," Sam yelled as he pulled a thick knot of crispy twenties out of one of the pant's pockets. "Man, if I knew this motherfucker was paid like this, I would of killed his ass as soon as we got to New York," he said laughing.

The living room had an all white leather sectional, with a glass coffee table positioned in front of it. John scanned the room looking for places where his stash could be hidden. Sam was content with the knot of twenties that he had in his hand, but John knew that there was more where that came from. He opened a closet door in the hallway that led to the bedroom. There were a bunch of coats, furs and expensive leathers inside, but no money. He found an old cigar box on a shelf in the closet, but it only had a 45-caliber piece in it, which he placed snugly in the waistband of his pants. While he searched, Sam was busy raiding the refrigerator, chomping down on an over cooked piece of leftover Porterhouse steak he had found.

John walked slowly towards the bedroom, cautiously taking in his environment. He admired a sexy picture of a scantily clad black woman that resembled one of *The Supremes*, hanging on the wall outside of the bathroom. He marveled in the expensive furnishings and décor. This was the type of life he dreamed of living when he came to New York.

The bedroom was beautifully painted in soft white. A white wooden canopy bed, a couple of glass night tables, an antique armoire and all white carpet helped accentuate the creamy white walls. John's socked feet sank into the thick carpet as he walked across the bedroom floor. He carefully checked the armoire and night tables, still searching for the stash, but only came across junk and other items of no interest. As he got down on his knees to check under the bed, a ruffling noise that originated from the closet caught his attention. He grabbed the revolver out of the back of his pants, and tiptoed slowly towards the door. Clutching his piece, he quickly swung the door open. A startled young black woman was lying on the floor, trying to conceal herself underneath some clothes she had pulled down off of the hangers. John cocked back the hammer and placed the gun to her temple. Her fear stricken body shook, as she stared at the barrel of the gun.

"Please...Please don't kill me," she begged, as tears began to flow down her face in a steady stream. John took his finger off the trigger and pulled the gun away from her head

"Get up," he yelled.

She stood up and stepped nervously out of the closet, still shivering uncontrollably as she clutched her pocketbook under her arm. Her caramel complexioned face looked no older than nineteen, but the tight peach satin dress that she wore highlighted her shapely and very mature body. She stood in the middle of the room squeezing her eyes shut so tightly that the veins were visible in her eyelids. John hit the light switch on the wall so he could get a better look at her. The light shined on her body, revealing her unblemished skin. John took a moment to stare, looking her up and down slowly, fully entranced by her beauty.

"Open up your eyes," John said in a soft but firm tone.

"I haven't seen your face mister. Please just go. I won't say nothing. I promise," she begged.

"I said open your fuckin' eyes," he commanded her in an authoritative tone. She reluctantly opened them, squinting uncomfortably as her pupils adjusted to the light in the room. John looked her up and down again, surveying her whole body. She had beautiful brown eyes that you could just get lost in if you stared too long. She gave off a subtle feel of innocence lost and maturity beyond her years. It was as if she didn't belong in this environment, or even to be involved in this lifestyle. He walked up to her and rudely snatched the pocketbook she had been clutching from underneath her armpit. Caught off guard, she jumped backwards in surprise. John rifled through lipstick and mascara, until he came across her wallet. She only had forty dollars inside, but he let that be, instead grabbing her driver's license and studying it closely.

"Who are you…Sarah *Buuggs*?" John asked.

"I'm Sarah Boggs"

"Sarah who?"

"Boggs."

"So, you're one of Hayward's bitches, huh?" He asked with a smirk on his face.

"I'm Hayward's girlfriend…If that's what you meant," she responded firmly. Sarah spoke in a very proper manner, obviously well versed and schooled.

"No, I said what I meant. You're one of the many bitches I've seen Hayward strutting around with. And now you just got yourself in some shit that you can't get out of."

"I told you mister, I don't even know who you are. Please, just let me go...I won't tell no one," she pleaded.

"Too late for all of that crying shit. You knew what you was gittin' into when you started fucking with a no good nigga like Hayward," he said in his slow southern drawl, pausing before continuing. "Besides, I feel like I know you very well now. I'm John Williams, the country motherfucker who just killed your boyfriend."

"And I'm Sam, the crazy motherfucker that's gonna kill you." Sam had just crept into the room after hearing his brother talking to someone from the kitchen. He had the sharecropper's knife in one hand and a bologna and cheese sandwich in the other. His eyes looked wild and without feeling. When Sara looked at him, tears immediately began to well up and burn her eyes again, as she sobbed uncontrollably. Her heart felt as if it had dropped into the pit of her stomach.

"Please...Oh, God please. Take whatever you want. The jewelry, the clothes...Take all the money. Just don't kill me."

"See, now we're talking. Where's the money?" John asked excitedly.

"It's in a safe behind that picture of the lion on the wall."

"And how we supposed to open that shit," Sam said, while still snacking down on his sandwich.

"I have the combination," she responded in a whisper.

"Damn, Hayward wasn't to hip wit his game, if he was just givin' out his safe combination to his freaks," John said sarcastically.

"I told you that I wasn't his bitch or his freak. I'm his girlfriend," she said firmly, while trying to fight back her tears. She gave John the safe combination, which was 12 left, 22 right and 14 left. After a few turns of the dial, he opened the safe revealing $20,000 in cash, a ledger, a black .45 and a couple of gold watches. He smiled at Sam, whose face lit up slightly when he saw the money.

"You know we gotta kill this bitch, right?" Sam said while looking at John, who was skimming through the pages of the ledger he had found.

"What's this shit all about?" He asked Sara, ignoring Sam's question while thumbing through the ledger.

"That's the ledger he used to keep track of people's bets and the numbers they picked," Sarah responded.

"So you mean to tell me that he was walking around like Rockerfeller, and he only got $20,000 in his safe?"

"Hayward only has one spot and plays some numbers for people on the street. He isn't big time, but he did some collecting each week for Woody."

"So, he wrote down every bet, huh?"

"Yeah, Woody made him do things that way after he slipped up and forgot who picked what numbers one week. Before then, he used to just memorize the numbers."

"Yeah? So, who the hell is Woody?"

"You don't know who Woody Davis is?" She asked surprisingly.

"If he knew who the fuck Woody Davis was, he wouldn't of asked that shit," Sam said sarcastically.

"Woody is the baddest motherfucker in Harlem. And you can bet he's gonna be coming over here tonight looking for his money and that book," she responded in an abrasive tone.

"Well that's even more the reason why we ain't leaving no witnesses," Sam said harshly, as he stared at her cunningly. Sara didn't flinch. By now, she was so scared that her body was numb with fear. His threats no longer affected her.

"How does this number thing work?" John asked inquisitively.

"You never played the numbers?" Sara asked in a surprised tone. She sensed his southern accent earlier, but was just beginning to realize that he wasn't really hip to the way things ran up north.

"Well, never mind... The game is pretty simple. Gamblers can pick up to three numbers. If their pick matches the last three digits of the total amount bet at the local track that day, then their number pays off at about six hundred to one," Sara said.

"I've played the numbers a couple of times, but I've only seen people play one number," Sam said. The talk of gambling had caught his attention.

"That's because the odds of winning are like one in one thousand when you bet against three numbers. When you bet one number the odds of winning are like 8 to 1, so naturally more people do that. But, the only thing is that the payoff is a lot less," she responded, her tone very confident.

"Damn, and they bringing in this much green, huh?" John asked.

"Woody makes over $100,000 a week. And like I said, he's gonna be over here any minute."

John looked directly into her eyes, as she stared back at him. She was by far the most beautiful girl he had ever seen.

"You gotta get outta town tonight," John said.

"John, we gotta kill this bitch. She jus gonna tell them who we is," Sam yelled out adamantly.

"If you gonna kill me, just get it over with then. Stop talking about it," Sara blurted out reflexively. She always had a problem with being quick with her tongue, but she regretted her latest outburst.

John cracked a smile and looked at her closely. "Ha ha ha…I like you. You got a big set of balls on you girl," he said admiringly. "No need to worry about losing your life no more though. I know that you ain't gonna tell nobody shit. Besides, if you're as smart as I think you are, you know that you are already dead. If Woody is as bad a motherfucker as you say he is, you ain't got a pot to piss in if you stay around here."

She looked him directly in his eyes, feeling an overwhelming sense of relief. She could tell he was a killer, but he didn't seem heartless like the other one, she thought to herself.

"Thank you," she whispered in relief. "I'll be on the next bus to Philly."

"You're making a big mistake John," Sam said, staring at her cunningly while tightly gripping the knife in his hand. He wanted to gut her like a trout.

"Nah, I trust her. We'll be alright," John said, as he turned and walked towards the door. Sarah bent down and quickly grabbed her bag off of the floor, placing the items that John had dumped out back inside. She frantically gathered her belongings, not wanting to stay a minute longer than she had to in the apartment with these killers. She followed John's trail towards the front door of the apartment.

"When you get back to Philly girl, no more messing with motherfuckers like Hayward," she thought to herself.

"I can't wait to see Momma's face when I—" Her thoughts were interrupted by the cold jagged edge of the knife blade that plunged into her lower back. She gasped in agony as Sam muffled her mouth from behind with his free hand, and then ripped the knife upwards, tearing through her skin and back muscles in a gutting fashion. The slight scream startled John, who instinctively turned around just as Sam laid her body down on the floor in the apartment. Her eyes stared blankly at the ceiling, as she jerked a few times before her body went completely limp.

John was furious as he rushed towards his little brother, who stared straight ahead without feeling. He grabbed him by the collar, as Sam who was still gripping the knife in his right hand coldly said, "The bitch would of ratted us out as soon as she got outta this fuckin' apartment John."

"I told her she could go Sam, I gave her my wor—"

"You know that bitch would have told John...you know that shit."

He loosened his grip on his brother's shirt, and walked back towards the living room. As cold and callous as his Sam's actions were, deep down he knew he was right. He was against killing innocent people, but he knew they couldn't leave any witnesses alive. He also knew that they had reached a point of no return. Their life course had been determined by two actions that took place in less than an hour.

♦

The chauffeur, Jimmy pulled the black Lincoln Town Car in front of Woody's Bar on 135th and seventh, parking directly in front of a fire hydrant. He nodded at Jive Talk, Woody's trusty lookout who always sat on a shoddy milk crate outside of the bar. Jive Talk was an old black war vet in his fifties. The deep wrinkles that were etched into his dark skin, were the effects of the hard life he lived. No matter what time of day it was, you could always count on Jive Talk to be outside reading a newspaper, or telling one of his exaggerated war stories.

Jive Talk nodded back to Jimmy in acknowledgment, then got up slowly and walked inside the bar. His old bones were aching from years of arthritis that had set in after he caught some shrapnel in his legs during the Second World War. A quick scan of the half empty bar room didn't reveal any loud boisterous bragging, or money being thrown around, so he knew that Woody must be upstairs in his office. He dreaded the pain he felt each time he had to walk up the flight of steps, but for fifty dollars a day, he had to do what he had to do. So he sucked it up, and slowly started walking up the steps at the pace of a tortoise.

Woody was a thirty five year old dark skinned black man with a medium sized build. He had worked his way from being a shoeshine boy, to controlling a significant piece of Harlem's numbers game. His empire was unique, because of the influence and protection provided by the Italians he was in bed with. Woody was very territorial, controlling several blocks at a time, with various businesses and numbers spots. At a time when most of Harlem was wide open for any hustler to make some green, he selfishly horded over his piece of the pie, strong arming any competitors that got in his way.

Woody stood in the middle of his modestly decorated office, resting his backside slightly up against his wooden desk. Never the modest type, his office walls were decorated with three pictures; one of him and James Brown, another with him and Diana Ross and finally one of him alone in a full-length mink coat. He looked over the fine young specimen that was standing in front of him, gazing into her large hazel eyes. She was a fine young hoe he had eyed earlier, sitting alone at the bar.

"So, what do you want baby girl? I mean talk is cheap and my time is money," Woody said in his deep baritone voice.

"You know what I want baby," She replied in a soft whisper. Smiling seductively, she slid the spaghetti straps of her silk dress off of her shoulders and let it fall down to her feet. Her nipples were perky on her tender caramel breasts. Woody gave a nod of approval as she walked over and slid down the zipper to his pants. She got down on her knees and slowly took his manhood into her mouth, bobbing up and down, applying the right amount of pressure with her tongue. Woody liked them young and had thought she was a virgin right out of high school when he saw her sitting at the bar only an hour ago. But the way she was sucking him off, he knew she had been around the track a couple of times.

"How does that feel baby," she said as she glanced her pretty hazel eyes up at him.

"Keep doing what you're doing," he said, as he pushed himself back into her mouth.

He was holding her head while moving his lower extremities in unison with her bobbing motion. After a few minutes his body began to jerk slightly, and he moaned loudly as he climaxed inside of her mouth. She smiled, realizing that she had made him come.

"Those are my babies you have floating around in your mouth," he said with a sarcastic grin on his face. "You better swallow them bad boys with care."

"Don't worry, they're in good hands," she said as she licked her thick lips seductively. Woody reached into his pocket and pulled a thick wad of fifties out of his pocket, spreading them across his desk as she looked on in awe.

"When was the last time you got fucked laying on top of two thousand dollars?" he asked in a cocky fashion. Without hesitation she got up on the desk lying spread eagle with her legs cocked wide open. Woody intensely stared at her perfect body as he prepared to insert himself inside of her.

"KnockKnockKnockKnockKnock"

The door rattled loudly as Jive Talk knocked on it with his bare knuckles. He didn't get a response so he knocked again even harder.

"Woody, you in there," he said placing his ear flush against the wooden door. "You there boss?"

"What's up, Jive?" He responded as he put his hardened penis back into his pants.

"Jimmy's waiting outside in the limo."

Woody just remembered that he was supposed to do a pick up from his man Hayward that night. He looked at the young piece of ass he had laying on his desk. So fine, so young. Without hesitation he said coldly, "Get up bitch, you gotta go."

"You just gonna leave me like this? I can do things with this pussy you ain't never seen baby," she said as she ran her hands over her body slowly and placed them between her thighs.

Woody looked her up and down again. He was getting harder by the second. She grabbed a fifty off of the desk and slid it over her naked body seductively. He loved pussy, but nothing was more important to him than his money. He was about to throw her out of his office, as he had done to so many other freaks, when she grabbed his manhood forcefully.

"I'm a ride you like a pony," she said as she helped him put his penis inside of her. She moaned excitedly as he pushed himself deeper and deeper into her tight vagina, feeling her get wetter and wetter. Then he stopped suddenly.

"What's wrong baby, you came already?" she asked.

"Shhh. Hold on a minute," he responded as he slowly walked over to the door of his office and opened it quickly. Jive Talk, who was visibly caught off guard, almost fell inside of the room. He had been trying to ease drop on Woody's sexual escapade, as he had successfully done so many times in the past, and didn't expect such a sudden interruption. Woody and the sexy female he left lying on his desk both stared at Jive Talk, making him feel even more embarrassed. He fixed the belt on his pants, which he had undone, before looking up at Woody.

"Is Melvin out there?" Woody asked the disheveled looking Jive Talk. Melvin was his right hand man, and his main muscle on the streets.

"I didn't see him."

"Do me a favor cat daddy and call him," he said, pausing between sentences. "Tell him that the limo is on its way to pick him up. He already knows where it's going."

"O.K. my man," Jive Talk responded.

"Now get outta here you dirty old motherfucker. I gots some business to take care of," he said as he looked back at his desk.

"O.K. Wood I'm going," Jive Talk responded as he quickly walked towards the stairs. He navigated the steps at a quicker pace than his old battered legs were accustomed to. He was out of breath when he reached the downstairs landing, but he willed himself to walk outside to the limo. Jimmy was draped in a tuxedo as usual, sitting on the hood of the black stretched limo smoothly taking pulls from a cigarette. He patiently waited as the old man walked towards him slowly, observing how disheveled he looked.

"Where's Woody?" Jimmy asked.

"He ain't comin. He want me n' you to pick up Melvin and head over to Hayward's pad," Jive Talk responded. He knew Woody hadn't told him that, but he was still feeling embarrassed by what just took place. He was determined not to be sitting around outside when the young lady upstairs left the bar.

"Whatever's clever," Jimmy said.

Jive Talk hopped into the back of the limo, as Jimmy got behind the steering wheel. If it had been Woody or Melvin he would have politely held the door open, but this was just Jive Talk he reasoned. He waited to hear the rear door slam shut before pulling away from the curb.

Melvin only lived a few blocks away which was convenient, because it was in the same direction as Hayward's apartment. The rain had let up, replaced instead by unwelcomed humidity. Jive Talk kept the window up, as the AC blew in his face, effectively cooling his sweaty body off. He reached into the mini bar, grabbed a bottle of Jack Daniels, and poured a little into a shot glass. Jimmy had one eye on the road and the other was peeking in the rear view mirror, staring past the lowered partition and looking directly at Jive Talk.

"You better not be drinking none of Woody's shit back there," he said harshly. He was still peeking at him with his right eye.

"Nah, man. I grabbed some of the cheap shit. I ain't gonna fuck with none of his good shit," Jive Talk said as he gulped down the golden liquid in the glass.

"I got those bottles marked. If you messed with the Jack Daniels, that's your ass," Jimmy said, glancing towards the road with both eyes as he took a turn onto Melvin's street.

"Stop worrying nigga. I don't even like whiskey."

After a few seconds passed, they arrived at Melvin's pad. There was a parking space in between Melvin's building and the apartment house next door. Jimmy pulled the limo up to the curb, placed it in park and let the engine run. A couple of minutes of dead silence passed, as they both sat quietly in the car.

"You gonna go get him or what?" Jimmy asked.

"Shiiittt, that's your job motherfucker. I ain't getting shit. You betta beep the motherfuckin' horn man. I got water in my knees and I walked up and down them steps fifteen motherfuckin' times today. And I got..."

Jimmy tuned Jive Talk out as he continued babbling on, drowning out his annoying voice by pressing down on the horn. The dimly lit block was unusually quiet. Jimmy looked at the darkly shrouded building and scanned the street, but he didn't see any movement or signs of anyone. Tired and worn out after a full day's work of chauffeuring people around, he didn't even notice the figure that crept out of the darkness of the alleyway between the two buildings.

Dressed in a black three-piece suit, he blended into the shadows with ease, as he slowly walked up to the driver's side of the limo. Jimmy slouched down in his seat and was just about to push the horn again, as Melvin quickly thrust his arm through the lowered car window and grabbed him around the throat.

"Press that horn again motherfucka', and that will be the last sound you hear," Melvin said forcefully in his raspy baritone voice.

"I'm...I'm sorry man. I thought—"

"Don't think motherfucka'," Melvin said as he let go of his neck, before walking to the back of the limo and yanking open the door.

Jive Talk sat slouched down in the back seat, feeling the effects of the 90-proof Jack Daniels he had gulped down. He slid across the leather seat in order to make room as Melvin stepped in the car. But, Melvin opted to sit his 250-pound frame in the middle of the seat located behind the partition, which faced directly towards Jive Talk. As he got comfortable, he flicked a switch that adjusted the lights in the back of the limo, making them very dim. With Melvin's midnight black complexioned skin, all Jive Talk could see was the whites of his eyes as he sat across from him.

"Whassup Jive? Didn't spect to see you tonight nigga," he said in a slow drawl.

"I'm cool. How, uh how about you?"

"I'm cool too. Cool as motherfuckin' ice," he said as he laughed slightly to himself, exposing his yellow teeth. His cackle sent chills up Jive Talk's spine, numbing the effects of the liquor and causing him to sober up quicker than he expected.

The tires squealed as Jimmy pulled the limo away from the curb and headed towards Hayward's crib, as Jive Talk sat staring downward towards the carpeting on the car's floor. He never looked directly at Melvin when they spoke, and always kept their conversations brief.

Melvin was a feared killer, who didn't need much help to set him off. When Woody was around, he kept him relatively in check. But, when you had to deal with him alone, there was no telling what could happen. Jive Talk could feel Melvin's stare, but he continued to look down nervously, as a patch of sweat began to form on his forehead.

The trip to Hayward's house seemed like an eternity for the old man, but before long, he felt the car slow down as Jimmy parked in front of Hayward's apartment.

"I'll be right back niggas," Melvin said as he opened the door and stepped out of the limo. Jive Talk nodded in acknowledgement. He watched as Melvin walked across the street and slipped into the building vestibule. As soon as he was out of sight, Jive Talk twisted the cap off of the Jack Daniels and took a long swig directly from the bottle.

"I can't stand that motherfucker," he mumbled under his breath, as he took another swig.

"Me neither," Jimmy responded as he turned around in his seat facing Jive Talk. "Pass that shit up here. I need a swig too."

At six-foot three, 250 pounds, Melvin was truly an intimidating specimen. A running back in high school, he always strived to stay fit and went out of his way to stay well conditioned. After taking only three strides, he quickly arrived at the top of the steps that led to Hayward's apartment, barely causing the stairs to creak. As he approached the apartment, he noticed that the wooden door was ajar. That was a little awkward, but he figured that Hayward probably left it open because he knew they were on their way.

He walked into the living room and took a quick look around. Everything seemed to be in order.

But, being someone who paid particular attention to detail, he noticed a minute red speck on the wooden floor. The floor had a coat of polyurethane that appeared to be a little smeared. Somebody had apparently tried to wipe it clean, but they missed a spot. He kneeled down and dabbed his pointer finger into the substance, and then he licked it off of the tip of his finger. It was definitely blood. He knew the taste of it very well.

"Hayward, what's up baby?" He yelled out. He failed to get a response, but he already had his black 45-caliber piece out of his waistband. Bent over slightly, he cautiously walked down the hallway that led to the bedroom.

"Hay, whatchu gonna do tonight?" He yelled out as he swiftly pulled open the closet door in the hallway with his left hand and pointed his pistol inside. He was ready to squeeze the trigger if there was any sign of movement, but there was no one in the closet. He crept slowly into the bedroom walking quietly on the balls of his feet. Even in hard bottomed shoes, he exhibited an excellent display of balance. His high school football coach would have been proud. It was the same technique he used when he would tiptoe along the sidelines attempting to get extra yardage out of a run.

Still standing in the hallway, he reached his left hand around and onto the bedroom wall until he found the light switch, which he flicked on. He heard no sudden movement or noise, so he slowly peeked around the corner into the bedroom. No one was in sight. Then he looked at the bed. There was a large lump, around the size of a body underneath a white comforter that had dark red bloodstains all over it.

Melvin started to walk towards the bed, but hesitated when he noticed the door to the wall safe hanging open. From his vantage point it looked empty. After bending down and peeking under the bed, Melvin got back into his offensive stance, walked over to the closet door and quickly swung it open. There were clothes strewn all over the floor, but nothing else. Satisfied that he had thoroughly checked the room, Melvin stood up straight and walked over to the bed. As he stood at the foot, he started to pull the comforter back as he said, "Damn, Hayward who the fuck did this to you nigga? Who killed my nigga?"

"You looking at him motherfucker!" John yelled out, as he quickly sprung out from under the bloody comforter, with his loaded piece pointed directly at Melvin's chest. Melvin's eyes widened in shock as he instinctively raised his gun towards John, just as the sound of bullets echoed throughout the room. Four hot slugs blasted through his chest plate, exiting through his back. Chunks of flesh from his heart and lungs sailed through the air, splattering the bedroom's creamy white walls.

Melvin's body flew backwards grossly as he managed to squeeze his trigger once, sending a bullet ripping through the bedroom floor as he fell. His body slid down the wall and sunk into the thick white carpet that quickly became saturated with red blood. John leaped from the bed and rushed over to him. He snatched the gun out of his limp hand and placed it in his own pocket.

"Too slow on the draw, nigga," John said as he leaned down and closed Melvin's eyelids shut. With his gun still in hand, John ran out of the apartment and down the steps. He put his shoes back on as he reached the downstairs landing, startled by a rumbling sound he heard behind the door of the first floor apartment.

"If anyone come out here, they gonna get their fuckin' head blown off," he yelled out, trying to disguise his voice as best he could.

The rumbling quickly ceased, as John opened the front door and slowly crept outside with his gun drawn. Jimmy had heard the gunshots, but he waited around to see if it was Melvin doing the shooting...or Melvin getting shot. By now, the rain had began again, graduating from light drizzle to a steady downpour. He squinted eyes, trying his best to see the individual who walked out of the building, to no avail. He couldn't see a face, but his instincts told him it wasn't Melvin. Scared and confused, he quickly slammed his foot on the gas pedal, speeding off down the wet street. John put his head down and walked off, slowly slipping off into the darkness.

CHAPTER 2

Woody got the disturbing call in his office, at approximately 12:30am. Jimmy was on the other end of the line completely out of breath and talking incoherently. Between his heavy breathing, he managed to explain what went down before he got off the phone, obviously shaken up by the events he had just experienced. Woody immediately sent a team of his killers over to Hayward's apartment, and they confirmed Jimmy's suspicions. Melvin had been savagely gunned down in a hail of bullets. The neighbors claimed they hadn't seen anything. They heard the sound of the gunshots echo throughout the building, and they said that they heard a man's voice, but that was about it.

What puzzled Woody even more was Hayward's disappearance. Ms. Smith, who lived on the first floor, thought she heard him come in around 9 o'clock, and then she heard the gunshots a couple of hours later. That was all she knew. So basically, he didn't have shit to go on.

"Why the hell would Hayward kill Melvin?" he thought to himself. It just didn't make any fuckin' sense. That was the thought he pondered the rest of the night as he struggled to get some sleep. Hayward had taken all of the money, and vanished with the ledger he used to track the number's bets.

"The motherfucker had the audacity to steal my money, and leave the bag in my hand to cover these fuckin' bets," he whispered scornfully under his breath.

It was like one final smack in the face. His blood began to boil inside of him as his anger grew. His most ruthless killers were out scouring every corner of the city, searching for that motherfucker. He couldn't wait to find the ungrateful son of a bitch, so he could cut his balls off himself.

Sergeant Glen Charles had rushed uptown to the scene of the crime, when he got the word that someone had murdered Melvin Walker, or Mad Money Mel as he was known on the streets. That was Woody's right hand man, and everyone knew that some major heat was going to come down on the streets as a result of his murder. But, he was even more perplexed by the fact that the word around town was that Hayward was the trigger-man. He knew Hayward personally, from various runs-ins they had back in the days when Hayward was a petty criminal, and Glen had just joined the force. Hayward was never known to be a murderer, and this whole cold-blooded killing didn't seem like it fit his M.O. at all.

Glen hurriedly drove his unmarked dark blue sedan down 8th avenue, heading towards midtown. He was running a little late for his scheduled meeting, so he swerved his car in and out of traffic trying to make up some time. His mind was consumed with thoughts of the crime scene he had visited earlier, and Hayward's whereabouts.

"Why had he disappeared all of a sudden?" He thought to himself. The fact that the murder had occurred in his own apartment, and his unexplainable absence had made him the prime suspect. But, something just didn't sit well with Glen. Hayward was always a flashy type of cat. It didn't make sense that he would leave his expensive chinchilla furs and plush Italian suits behind, if he had indeed left town. Hell, he didn't even take all of his jewelry with him.

Still rushing, Glen ran through a red light, barely missing a pedestrian who was aggressively standing in the crosswalk. The talk on the streets was quieter than Glen had ever experienced during his fifteen years on the force. He was a highly respected Black officer who grew up in the community, and was known for giving even the most notorious criminals a pretty fair shake. Because of this, he had developed some pretty good contacts that he could always turn to for the low down. But unfortunately, even they had no leads in regards to Melvin's murder.

When he reached 39th street, Glen hurriedly pulled his car over to the curb. The car jerked awkwardly as he threw it in park, before he trotted into a modest looking diner that was located on the corner. The twenty-four hour diner was nestled between an antique gift shop and a nickel and dime store that sold costume jewelry and various trinkets. Glen liked meeting here, because there were only eight booths with low partitions. He could easily see everyone and everything that was going on around him no matter where he sat.

Surveying the scene, he scanned the faces of the four patrons that sat in the various booths, as he walked by. He was looking for anyone or anything out of place. Glen had good intuition and always used it to his advantage. After scanning the interior for a half a minute, he was convinced that nothing was out of the ordinary.

The diner was rarely packed, but today it was unusually slow even for a weeknight. As he made way to his usual table, located towards the rear of the diner he said, "Hello," to Jeannie. Jeannie was a shapely white waitress in her early forties, who normally worked weeknights. The years had been kind to Jeannie, blessing her with wrinkle free skin and no blotches. He'd known her for at least a decade, and always tipped her well whenever he stopped by for a cup of hot java.

Paul Weatherspoon was already sitting in the cramped booth, waiting impatiently for Glen. He had downed his second cup of black coffee, and was jittery from the rush of caffeine. Glen politely shook Weatherspoon's hand as he sat down, barely able to see his eyes, which were hidden beneath the brim of his blue New York Yankee's baseball cap. There was undeniable tension in the air, which Glen felt immediately. As Weatherspoon took a long sip from his coffee mug, he involuntarily tapped the pointer finger of his right hand nervously on the table.

"How's it going Paul," Glen asked as he poured a heaping spoon of sugar into the cup of coffee in front of him. Jeannie had left it at the table minutes earlier, in anticipation of his arrival.

"It's going," Weatherspoon responded. His words were weak, his voice trailed off noticeably.

Glen leaned forward, resting his elbows on the table. "Yeah, I got you man. It ain't even worth complaining about, cause don't nobody gives a fuck really. Right?"

"I can't take this shit no more man," Weatherspoon blurted out, as he slammed the palm of his right hand forcefully onto the wooden table. Startled, Glen's coffee spilled and the silverware made a loud clanking noise, alarming the patrons at the other tables.

Reflexively Glen reached out and pressed the palm of his right hand forcefully against Weatherspoon's chest.

"Relax, Paul. Just fuckin' relax," Glen said sternly, as he pulled a white monogrammed handkerchief out of his jacket pocket and used it to wipe the hot coffee off of the table.

He turned and scanned the diner again, catching the concerned stares of some people who were looking on nosily. As their eyes met, the nosey patrons looked away embarrassingly, resuming the activities they were participating in before the awkward disturbance took place. Glen focused his attention back on Weatherspoon. He could see that this assignment was visibly taking its toll on his young informant, but this was the first time he actually saw him lose his composure. He didn't want to risk losing all of the progress they had made over the last year. He was certain that he was very close to making an arrest soon.

All of these thoughts ran through his mind, but he put them aside in order to address Weatherspoon and hopefully put his mind at ease. He knew he had to say something to help regain his confidence.

"Paul, what the hell is wrong with you? Have you lost your fuckin' mind," Glen yelled out sternly.

He was never one to mince his words or beat around the bush. So, even when he tried to show compassion, he came across bluntly and to the point.

A tear slowly ran down Weatherspoon's weathered face, from his bloodshot red eyes that were no longer hidden beneath his cap. The dark skinned man's bottom lip quivered uncontrollably as he struggled to articulate his thoughts.

"I just can't take this shit no more Glen," he said, pausing to take another sip of his coffee. "I don't feel right about this shit man. It's not right. Haven't I given you enough already? I mean, this is bullshit!"

Glen looked at his young companion, and immediately envisioned himself ten years ago during his first tough assignment on the force. He too had been pushed to his emotional limit, nearly reaching his breaking point. But, he rose to the occasion, and because of that early bout with adversity, he was a better cop today. So, he partly felt for Weatherspoon. But on the other hand, Weatherspoon was a low down dirty marijuana smoking numbers runner and a thief. Their situations were quite different from one another. Glen glanced upwards, giving him a once over before spitting out a scathing spiel.

"I should have locked your monkey ass up and thrown away the key, you ungrateful nigga!"

"But, Glen I—"

"Don't but Glen me. There's no statute of limitations on armed robbery you dumb sonofabitch. I could run your ass in right now," he said, pausing to look around the diner before continuing.

"Do you see all the shit that's going on in the streets? I know you had to have heard something.

Shit is falling apart at the seams, and that whole organization is going to fall apart. When that shit happens, I need you to be there. After that, you don't have to worry about meeting me at this fuckin' diner anymore. That's when you see the fruits of all your hard labor, and you can go back to your old miserable life. Do you understand?" Glen asked in an authoritative manner.

Weatherspoon was nervous and sweating profusely. He wiped his forehead with the back of his hand before saying, "It's hard Glen...it's fuckin hard. I've been doing this shit for almost a year now, and I feel like I'm dying inside. I'm starting to forget who the fuck I really am."

Jeannie walked over to the table and filled both of their cups up to the brim with some freshly brewed coffee. Glen cracked a smile at her, and she smiled back teasing him with her eyes as she asked, "Do you guys want anything to eat?"

"What I'm hungry for ain't on the menu," Glen said flirtatiously, giggling lightly to himself while he cracked a sly grin.

Jeannie smiled back and said, "Well just let me know if you change your mind," before walking off to help another patron. She purposely switched her hips, knowing that Glen's eyes were planted on her voluptuous backside, as it jiggled noticeably underneath her light blue skirt. She had quite a body for a white woman, and liked to flaunt it seductively.

Glen's eyes remained glued to her for a few seconds, and then without missing a beat he continued talking to Weatherspoon. "Maybe it's a good thing that you're forgetting who you really are, because the old you wasn't worth shit," he said, breaking his stare in order to finish his thought. "I'm giving you a chance to make a difference son. There are good guys and there are motherfuckin' bad guys. What the fuck are you? I know what side I'm on, but you have to make the choice son."

"I know what side I'm on too Glen, but this shit is just hard."

"Nobody said that the shit would be easy. But, the reward is great. After this is over, you're free to live your life with no obligations hanging over your head. You've paid your debt to society by helping me clean that filth off of the street," Glen said convincingly.

He was always a great motivator and exceptionally good at convincing others to do tough things solely for his own selfish benefit. He idolized Adam Clayton Powell, and planned on using his orating skills after he retired from the force, to land a job on the City Council.

"You're right Glen...you're fuckin' right," Weatherspoon said, speaking in a barely audible whisper. " It's only a little while longer now. Shit's about to hit the fan, and this'll be all over," he said, conveying a slight degree of confidence in his voice that had been missing only minutes earlier.

"I know I'm right," Glen said as he patted Weatherspoon lightly on the shoulder. "Now, drink your coffee and give me the rundown on what's going on."

The two men sat in the diner talking for another half an hour before parting ways. As always, Glen left the diner first, followed ten minutes later by Weatherspoon who walked out and headed quickly in the opposite direction. Glen always stayed around discreetly watching Weatherspoon through his binoculars, until he saw him safely drive off in his car.

Convinced that Weatherspoon had gone about his business unharmed and unnoticed, Glen pulled a whiskey flask out of the inner pocket of his navy colored blazer, and took a quick gulp. He had too much riding on this kid to let him have a nervous breakdown now. His dreams of obtaining a job on the City Council depended on his well-being. He'd be damned if he was going to let his plan fall apart at the seams now.

◆

It was early Sunday morning, and an enthusiastic crowd of approximately seventy-five onlookers were gathered around a man standing atop a soapbox on the corner of Lenox Ave and 135th street. This famous corner was known as *the crossroads of the black world*. The tall slim dark-skinned black man didn't have a microphone, nor did he need one. When he spoke, his overpowering voice traveled, easily reaching the ears of everyone in attendance.

"Brothers and sisters, you've been suffering from a bad case of spiritual sickness. The white man has been breeding you like a wild pack of animals in the ghettos around the world. You don't trust your own brother, because you've been trained to be a white man lover. But, I'm here to free you from the mental captivity that your ignorance has you bound by, and set your caged intelligence free. All praise is due to Allah!"

"All praise is due to Allah!" The crowd responded resoundingly.

After his powerful speech, the gentleman walked amongst the crowd. He shook hands and hugged people, as a group of men that were with him handed out leaflets that said, *"The Black Muslims"* on them. John stayed back and observed the whole spectacle that was taking place in front of his eyes. He was amazed at the control the speaker had over the crowd. His words were more powerful than any knife or gun could ever be, he thought. John was truly amazed.

He mingled amongst the crowd, steadily moving forward, trying to get closer to the man who had just dazzled the audience. After spending several minutes squeezing in between the men and women that were gathered about, he finally reached the speaker. His back was facing John, as he shook a young lady's hand and kissed a young boy on the forehead.

"Excuse me," John said as he tapped the speaker lightly on his shoulder. The man turned around with his hand already extended.

"Peace be upon you Black man," he said warmly. John stared at him closely, noticing that the man was also looking back at him as if they knew each other from somewhere. John was silent, just staring oddly, until he caught the face.

"Bubba?" John asked inquisitively. "Bubba, is that you?"

"Johnny...Johnny Williams," he responded in astonishment, as he hugged John tightly.

"Damn, Bubba I can't believe that that's you," John said excitedly.

"I changed my name. I'm Bilal now...Bilal X," he said before continuing. "I can't believe it's you! Man, we got a lot of catching up to do Johnny."

They walked down a couple of blocks to a local soul food restaurant named, "*Rubie's Diner*". The interior was very spacious, with light colored paneled walls and square wooden tables neatly juxtaposed in three rows. A young waitress in her early twenties ushered John and Bilal to a table in the back room away from the other patrons, and politely seated them. Bilal knew the restaurant owners well, and they always arranged for him to have the same table. Two intimidating black men in black suits, white dress shirts and black bowties, that had flanked Bilal during his speech, were escorted to a separate table that was closer to the restaurant's entrance. They kept a watchful eye on John as he spoke to Bilal...one of them more intensively than the other.

"I can't believe you're here in Harlem, John. What brought you up here?"

"Me and Sam been up here for a couple of months now, just looking for some new opportunities. You know? If we stayed in Williston, Sam was gonna either end up dead or locked up. I had to get him out of there."

"Little Skeeter was always into sumthin'. I can't believe he's up here too. Man, this is unreal."

"Damn, I know Bubba...Uh, I mean Bilal. I can't believe I ran into you. I mean, I kept hearing rumors that *you* were dead or locked up," John said, before taking a sip of water from his glass.

"I was John. I was mentally imprisoned and spiritually dead for over twenty years," Bilal said, with the same confidence and authority he projected during his speech earlier.

John looked him over closely. Still astonished, he couldn't believe his eyes. Bubba had been his best friend growing up. They had done everything together. When times were rough, they even performed petty robberies outside of the local juke joints together. They were inseparable growing up, but then one day eight years ago, Bubba's family just up and moved to Chicago. John hadn't heard from him since. Through word of mouth, he had found out that Bubba had been arrested. But then, he also heard rumors that he had been gunned down by some Chicago gangsters. So, he really didn't know what to believe.

Bubba was only a year older than John, but he looked like he had him by at least two or three years easily. When they were younger, he was always able to pass for a grown man because of the hairy full beard that he kept. But, that was gone now. His face was shaven clean, and Bubba, now known as Bilal, barely resembled the teen that used to refer to John as his brother.

Bilal was sharply dressed to kill in an all black suit, a perfectly starched white shirt, and shiny gold cufflinks. Sitting across from Bilal, John felt relieved that he took the time to pick up some new wears first thing that morning. He would have hated to run into his old friend Bubba wearing the ragged threads he had on the night before.

"So, what's this all about Bilal?" John asked inquisitively.

"What do you mean?" Bilal responded.

"I mean," John said, before pausing and leaning across the table to get closer to Bilal. Now talking in a whisper he said, "I have to give it to you Bubba. This has got to be the best scam you've ever come up with. How the hell did you think this one up?"

Bilal laughed, and took a sip from his water before he responded. "John, this isn't a scam. You're looking at the real deal. I'm no longer Bubba, as the slave master would have me be. I'm Bilal X," he said before continuing. "Man, we really do have a lot of catching up to do Johnny."

"I can respect that. I'm just amazed, you know. This is a lot to digest at once."

"I know what you mean, but it's real. They say the truth is hard to swallow, but I've learned that it's easier to digest than the lies I've been fed."

"When did all of this take place? I mean the whole transformation."

"When I was locked in that can in Chicago. I was evil tempered and confused. A Muslim brother that was serving time with me helped me find Islam, and my true self...It changed my life."

"I'd say," John said sarcastically.

"Forget you, John," Bilal responded while laughing.

"Listen...To the rest of these people you may be like the Martin Luther King of the ghetto and shit, but you always gonna be plain ole' Bubba to me," John said laughing hysterically. Bilal punched him in the shoulder, as he broke out into a loud laughter as well.

The pretty waitress who had seated them earlier, returned with two plates of scrambled eggs, corned beef hash and cheese grits, which she placed down on the table. She came back a few minutes later with two glasses of freshly squeezed orange juice.

"Damn, that's what I call service. You don't even have to tell them what you want," John said, pausing to talk between eating. He had dug in as soon as the waitress left the plate on the table.

"I eat here often enough, so they know me."

"Food is damn good here too."

"Yeah, reminds me of the down home cooking from the south," Bilal said. His facial expression changing, as a thought seemed to come to mind. "Speaking of the south, how's your mom doing? She sure could throw down in the kitchen."

"Mom passed on almost two years ago now. You know, it was the cancer. It ate right through her," John responded in a low whisper.

"Damn, I'm sorry to hear that man. I'm real sorry to hear that. So, you and Sam are all alone then, huh?"

"Yep. All we got is each other."

"And what's up with your big brother Willie?"

"Willie is officially a member of the armed forces. He's stationed over in Korea," John responded.

"Damn, they got him over there fighting the white man's war."

"Yep."

"So, what are you going to do with yourself Johnny? Huh? You should think about joining the cause. I could use a good brother like you by my side," Bilal said in a serious tone.

"So, you'd be Martin and I'd be like Jesse right?"

"Nah, you'd be like the brother you always were to me. Just like old times."

"I can't fuck with the bow tie, no ham hock no pig feet movement right now," John said, pausing as he gathered his thoughts. "No disrespect, but I'm trying to do some other things right now."

"Like what?"

"You ever heard of a dude named Woody Davis?"

"Yeah, he's a hustler and numbers banker who has our people wasting their money on false hope, instead of investing back into their own community."

"Yep, that's him. Say, do you know where I can find him?"

"He has a nightspot on 135th. Why do you ask? Woody's a shady character."

"Just curious."

"Man, you ain't never been just curious about nothing."

"Nah, I heard he was the man to see to play the numbers...that's it."

"Johnny, you ain't changed a bit. I could always tell when you were lying. But in any case, I know that he spends a lot of time at that nightspot."

"That's good to hear. Maybe I'll pay him a visit someday."

Bilal had just finished eating his food, when the waitress came back over with two saucers of sweet potato pie. Bilal told her, "Thanks," but he was too full to eat it. Without hesitation, John gladly reached over and took the pie off of his hands.

"Oh yeah, did you know that Doc Wilson and his brother Curtis are up here too?" Bilal asked John.

"No way. Not the crazy ass Wilson brothers," John responded excitedly.

"Yep, they're still crazy as all hell too. But, they weren't doing too good last time I saw them," Bilal responded.

"Really? Damn, I'm sorry to hear that."

"Yeah man, they live in a rundown apartment over on 113th. You should go see them some day."

"I'm a definitely do that real soon."

They both stood up from the table, and Bilal walked over to John and gave him a big hug. He handed him a piece of paper that he had scribbled his name and number on earlier.

"Give me a call in a couple of days. Maybe we can do dinner or something," Bilal said.

John put the paper in his pants pocket and said, "Sounds like a plan, my man."

"Peace be upon you. As my Muslim brothers would say," Bilal said as he held his hand towards John. John grabbed it firmly and shook it.

"Yeah, peace and hair grease to you too," John said as he walked towards the restaurant door exiting out onto the sidewalk still laughing quietly to himself. Bilal's bodyguards looked on coldly as he exited the establishment.

CHAPTER 3

Woody sat behind the desk in his oversized leather office chair, sipping on a warm glass of Jack Daniels. He hadn't slept a lick since he heard the news from Jimmy, but his body was running off of pure adrenalin. It had been almost twelve hours, and still nobody had seen Hayward or heard anything about his whereabouts. As he sat there staring outward with unfeeling eyes, he felt himself getting angrier by the minute. Melvin was his main man. They started running together when they were back in high school, and had been tight ever since.

On the other hand, Hayward just moved into the neighborhood five years ago. He was eight years younger than Woody, but mature for his age and cool as hell. They immediately clicked when they met. Woody took him under his wings, showing him the ropes like a big brother. But in less than twenty-four hours, he had lost his best friend and the young protégé he trusted with his life, was on the run. As Woody took another sip of Jack Daniels, savoring the taste in his mouth momentarily, he swore that he would avenge Melvin's death. He made a personal vow to kill that motherfucker Hayward.

"So, you have no idea where Hayward is? I mean, he just up and disappeared without telling his bitch nothing, huh?" Woody asked, staring directly into her eyes.

Melba sat on the other side of the desk, with her back slumped down in an uncomfortable wooden chair. She was one of Hayward's freaks, that he messed around with and brought to the bar every so often. Woody had sent his enforcer Spence over to pick up one of Hayward's other freaks, Sarah earlier. When she couldn't be found, he drove over to the east side and snatched up Melba. Woody had been probing her, asking the same questions for the past two hours. She sat across from him visibly exhausted and mentally drained.

"He didn't tell me nothing, Woody. Maybe...uh...maybe he didn't rob you and kill Melvin. Maybe he got kidnapped, or maybe he got wounded by the killers and he's hiding out until—" Woody interrupted her rudely.

"And maybe I'm the black Santa Claus bitch," he said scornfully before continuing. "I always thought you were a cool young freak. Not the cutest bitch, but you had a nice ass and a good set of tits. But you see, my patience is growing thin."

"Woody, I don't know shit. If I knew something, don't you think I woulda told you already? I know you're not stupid. I wouldn't lie to you. You know I'm not his only girl," Melba said pleadingly.

Woody knew that Hayward had plenty of bitches, but his main two hoes were Sarah and Melba. If any of his bitches knew something, it would be one of these two, and Sarah was missing also.

"So, you just happened to have a train ticket to D.C., the same day Hayward fuckin' disappears huh?"

She glanced downward, not wanting to make eye contact with Woody. She knew that her actions looked suspicious. Her first reaction when she heard that Hayward killed Melvin, was to get outta town as quickly as possible. She didn't know where Hayward was, but her instincts told her that shit was gonna hit the fan.

Melba exhaled slowly before she replied, "I told you I was going to visit my aunt. She's sick and I wanted to see her. Damn, what do I have to say to make you believe me? What do I have to—"

In one motion, Woody put his drink down on the desk and back slapped her with all the force he could muster. Melba's black wig flew across the room as she fell off of the chair onto the hard floor.

She lay in pain holding her throbbing face as tears poured out of her eyes. She put her tongue to the corner of her mouth, tasting the bitter tang of blood that flowed freely from a cut caused by one of Woody's gold rings.

"I told you I'm not the nigga to be fucked with bitch," Woody yelled out angrily, before he rolled the sleeves of his dress shirt up to his elbows. His eyes looked deranged as he walked from behind the desk, and made way towards Melba. She balled herself up into the fetal position, stricken with fear and barely able to move. Knots began to form in her stomach, as she braced herself in anticipation of him letting loose on her again.

"*Knockknockknock.*" the rattling at the door was like music to Melba's ears. Woody stopped in his tracks, as his attention shifted towards the door.

"Who is it?" Woody asked in a harsh tone.

"It's Jive Talk."

"Go away nigga, I'm busy."

"There's somebody here to see you about a numbers bet."

"Look, tell that motherfucker to go away. I'm not covering anymore of Hayward's bets. You tell them to go find that motherfucker if they want their bread."

There was a couple of seconds of silence, while Jive Talk waited before hesitantly saying, "That's just it boss. The guy downstairs claims that he just saw Hayward, and he told him to come see you."

◆

John stood confidently in front of the bar, checking himself out in the full size brass framed mirror that hung from the wall. He had already ordered a rum and coke, which he sipped on slowly, as he stood admiring his tall lanky frame in the mirror. He had lost a whole lot of weight, but was amazed at what an expensive set of threads could do for an individual. He left a five-dollar tip for the bartender, who cracked an appreciative smile when he retrieved the dough. He figured the least he could do was spread some of Woody's money around.

The bar was mostly empty...at least there were none of the regular patrons around. The old man who had introduced himself to John as Jive Talk, came back into the room and sat on one of the barstools. He immediately began complaining about his ailing knees and the war. John found him entertaining, and listened closely to his animated tales as he waited for Woody.

There were also three other guys that were sitting around the bar, trying their best to look intimidating. John assumed that they were Woody's hired guns. One of which had patted him down as soon as he stepped into the bar. John wasn't packing though, he left his piece in the car. Besides, he didn't come here to kill Woody, he was only making this visit to engage in conversation. He was real excited about finally meeting the baddest motherfucker this side of Harlem, as Woody had been described.

John sat at the bar waiting patiently, and after a few minutes had passed, Woody and his bodyguard Spence walked into the room. John looked directly into their eyes, sizing both of them up. He always felt that you could tell a lot about an individual by looking into their eyes...the gateway to the soul. Woody had a mean and intimidating scowl, but John wasn't the least bit impressed. He'd been in the presence of plenty of coldhearted killers. Tough demeanors didn't really move him.

"What can I do for you?" Woody asked. He had positioned himself directly in front of John with his arms crossed and resting on his chest.

"Are you Woody?" John asked.

"It's according to who's asking?" Woody responded.

"I'm John. John Williams."

"And what can I help you with Mr. Williams?"

"My numbers hit yesterday, and I'm here to collect my money."

"Oh, really," Woody said, giggling slightly to himself. "I don't recall you playing shit with me."

"Actually, I played with your man Hayward. And when I saw him a couple of hours ago, he told me to see you for my money."

"Well, you got the wrong nigga. I don't pay no other man's debts. But, maybe I can straighten this misunderstanding out with Hayward. Where did you see him?"

"Why do you ask? I mean, that nigga works for you, right?"

Woody lightly tapped Spence on his side, as he let out a sinister laugh. "I see we got us a little smart ass country motherfucker here," he said sarcastically.

"All I want is my money," John responded.

"Then your best bet is just to tell me where you seen him at?"

"I seen him up on 145th street."

Agitated, Woody's attention shifted towards Spence. "How the fuck is this nigga Hayward just roaming up and down 145th street, when I'm supposed to have the whole city out looking for his ass?"

Dumbfounded, Spence just shrugged his shoulders. Woody rolled his eyes in disgust, and looked back towards John.

"Cool. Come see me in a couple of days. If I catch up with Hayward, I'll get your money, minus a small finder's fee of course," Woody said.

"Yeah, o.k." John said, as he took a long sip from his drink.

Woody leaned over to Spence, and whispered something into his ear. Spence nodded in acknowledgment, before walking out of the front door of the bar. Shortly afterwards, Woody motioned his hand towards Jive Talk and said, "Go bring Melba down here for me."

A couple of minutes passed, before Jive Talk returned.

"Here she is, boss." Jive Talk said, cracking a smile.

Melba stood in the middle of the floor and scanned the room. She looked dejected and overwhelmed with pain.

"Melba, it seems like your boyfriend has mysteriously reappeared," Woody said sarcastically.

"Oh, thank God. I told you he wouldn't rob you. There must be some misunderstanding," Melba replied excitedly.

"Yeah, misunderstanding alright. But, don't worry, shit's about to be cleared up real soon," Woody said coldly.

Spence walked back into the bar and motioned for Melba to come over to him. Confused, she looked over to Woody for some direction.

"Go on baby. You done well. My man Spence is gonna put you up in a nice room, while I settle this *misunderstanding* between me and Hayward," Woody said unconvincingly.

Melba hesitantly turned and walked out the door behind Spence, her eyes welling up with tears. John calmly finished up his drink, pretending to be oblivious to what was going on inside the bar. Jive Talk hobbled back into the room out of breath. He had been watching Melba walk to the car.

"Damn, that Melba sure got a walk on her," Jive Talk said.

"Yeah, she got a nice little ass and firm set of tits on her. I hope you took some time and got yourself a nice long look though," Woody responded coldly.

"Why you say that Wood?"

Woody leaned in closely to Jive Talk, cracking a sinister grin as he whispered softly into his ear, "Cause the next time you see that bitch, she'll be in a casket."

CHAPTER 4

Sam sat patiently in the bleachers that overlooked the basketball court, sipping from his Coca-Cola soda pop bottle and eating some greasy chips, as he waited for his brother John to join him. He was at the King Tower's basketball tournament, looking on observantly from his seat. A few hours earlier he had ditched an old Buick he had stolen, in a vacant lot next to a dilapidated building. Hayward Jones and his girlfriend Sarah's decaying bodies were locked securely in the trunk of the vehicle.

The weather was very pleasant outside. Bright sunrays were beaming down through the clouds causing a slight heat wave, but the crowd that flooded the park wasn't the least bit fazed. They were too entranced by the magical moves a young man they affectionately called, Black Jesus was making on the court. He was putting on an incredible exhibition of ball handling skills, as he dribbled between his legs, studder-stepped, faked a pass to his left and finished off with a sweet finger roll that swished in the basket...all net. The crowd went crazy, chanting his name out loudly, "Black Jesus...Black Jesus...Black Jesus!!!"

Sam was left in awe by the game, but even more engrossed by the amount of dead presidents that were exchanging hands from the various bets that were taking place. He loved gambling and his favorite fragrance was the scent of new money. He made a vow to himself to never let him or his brother find themselves in the same predicament they were in just yesterday. *Out of luck, out of cash and out of food.* His frigid heart didn't care who he had to rob or murder. He'd be damned if he ever lived that way again.

John had purposely took the time to talk to him after the killings, concerned that within time the severity of the events that recently transpired would began to weigh on him. But to the contrary, Sam was more focused than ever. Hayward and Sarah's murders had left him unmoved and unfeeling. In his mind, that nigga had that shit coming. And as for his bitch, she knew the rules of the game. Sometimes you gotta pay when you play.

Quietly he sat eavesdropping, trying to take in everything that was going on around him.

"I could easily rob one of these motherfuckers," he thought to himself, as he stared at a couple of cats in fancy suits flashing their mitt. The cold steel of the .38 he had tucked snugly into the belt line of his pants earlier, was pressed uncomfortably against his back.

Before he knew it, the sun was starting to set and the game was wrapping up. He glanced down at the gold watch he had bought himself earlier in the day. John was supposed to meet him over an hour ago, and he still wasn't there. His instincts had him feeling uncomfortable and awkward, ever since

John told him that he was going over to Woody's bar alone. He never liked for them to be separated from one another, and now he wished that he had followed his gut feeling and went with him.

Earlier in the day he had done some inquiring on his own, and the overall consensus was that Woody was a vicious and feared killer on the streets. He struggled to put his worries aside, trying to convince himself that John knew how to handle his business on his own. He waited fifteen more minutes, and then he got up and made his way out of the park. They were supposed to try and find the Wilson brothers together, but since John obviously got caught up, Sam figured he might as well head over to their pad on his own. Besides, he hadn't seen those crazy ass country boys in years, and he was looking forward to catching up with them.

He hailed a cab, and told the driver to head over to 113th. Yesterday, he was starving and broke. In his wildest dreams, he couldn't have imagined hopping a cab anywhere, but now he could afford to travel in "style".

As they drove, he pulled a cigarette out of his pocket, lit it up and took a couple of long pulls as he stared out of the window. The beautiful women who were scattered about caught his eye. The cab driver skillfully drove in and out of traffic, and within a few minutes, they had arrived at his destination. Children were playing hopscotch on the sidewalk and getting cooled off by the fresh water shooting out of a nearby hydrant.

The cab driver parked safely out of the reach of the water and told Sam, "That will be $2.00." Sam slid him a five-dollar bill, and let him keep the change, before he stepped out of the cab.

The old tenement building was visibly run down, and looked to be inhabited by squatters and junkies. Sam ran his hand across his beltline, making certain that his .38 caliber piece was secure and within reach. After verifying, he confidently opened the front door and stepped into the abandoned lobby. A mouse swiftly ran across the dirty tiled floor, before vanishing into a crack in the wall underneath a rusty radiator. To Sam's left was a ragged staircase, which he used to get up to the second floor.

The building looked bigger from the outside, but surprisingly, there were only two apartments on each floor. Sam walked halfway down the narrow hallway and knocked on the door that was to his right. It wasn't closed tightly, so it easily swung open as his knuckles rattled against it.

"Hello," Sam yelled out. His voice echoing throughout the empty interior. Seconds passed by, and Sam was about to head towards the apartment on the opposite side of the hallway when somebody said, "Who you want maaan?"

Sam could recognize the distinctive southern drawl anywhere.

"Killer Curt Wilson! What's going on my man?" Sam yelled out excitedly, as he walked inside the apartment and gave him a hug. Curt was a couple of years older than Sam, but you'd never know it by talking to him. His broken English was due to the fact that he had never spent a day of his life in a classroom. However, Curt was very well trained in the streets, and adept in the art of committing murder and mayhem.

"Skeeter! What in the hell is ya doing chair?" Curt asked surprisingly, with a wide grin on his face.

The tight fitting t-shirt and boxer shorts he wore were dingy and reeked of alcohol and sweat. His round belly protruded outwards, almost fully exposed beneath the small shirt..

"Man, I'm just trying to get an honest day's pay, for an honest day of work in the big city," Sam responded sarcastically.

"Shoot…*whatamIawoodorwhat?* You ain't never did no honest shit in your whole life. I ain't fittin' believe you done changed now," Curt said laughing, exposing his rotten yellow teeth.

"I'm serious. I'm a businessman now, Curt." Sam responded with a huge smile on his face.

"Like I done said…*whatamIawoodorwhat?* Where ya done got ya dat dear fancy suit from, Skeet?"

"A good business deal. As a matter of fact, that's why I'm here. I wanted to see if you and Doc want to get in on my new business venture. Where's Doc at anyway?"

"He'll be right back. He just went out chair fittin to fetch'm somthin' to eat,"

"Damn! My man Killer Curt. You still know how to handle a .45?"

"Shhiiittt! I can shoot da tail off a donkey, and da white off a honky," Curt said as he broke out into laughter.

The apartment door made a creaking noise as it swung open, remaining ajar for a few seconds before Doc slowly strolled in. He was slimmer than Sam remembered, but his facial features still looked the same. Dark skinned and tall, Doc got his nickname from being cold-blooded like his idol Doc Holiday, and also for being a smooth operator with the ladies. His eyes lit up when he saw Sam.

"Skeeter? What the hell are you doing here?"

"He fittin' to start some shit up in dis here town," Curt said sarcastically.

"Oh yeah? What you got up your fancy ole sleeves? Lookin' all sharp and shit. What is that silk?" Doc asked.

"Something like that. Imported fine shit, you dig?" Sam responded.

"N' where you done got you some money for a silken shirt from?" Curtis said.

"You know how we used to roll over them drunks back home?" Sam asked.

"Yes sir. Do I," Doc replied.

"Well we stepped it up a bit. Me and John is rolling over number runners now," Sam said sternly.

"*WhatamIawoodorwhat?*" Curtis said.

"How can we get in on this? Man, we struggling. We can't buy a break up here," Doc said as he slammed his right fist into the palm of his left hand. A vein was visibly protruding out of the left side of his forehead as his facial expression became serious.

"That's what I came here for. I need your help with a little sumthin'. This shit is gonna be like taking candy from a baby," Sam said pausing before continuing his thought. "Any of you broke motherfuckers got a ride?"

"Doc gots him a car, but it ain't got no insurance and it's low on gas," Curtis said.

"As long as it runs, I'll take care of the gas. We may hafta use your ride if John don't show up soon. We got some New York niggas to rob tonight," Sam said.

"All you have to do is say the word," Doc said as he pulled his shiny .45-caliber pistol out of his waistband and cracked a sinister grin. Like John, Sam and several others who traveled up from the south, Doc had been smacked in the face with a dose of reality when he arrived in New York with his brother Curt. No matter how hard he tried to get ahead, doors were continuously being slammed in his face. This run in with Sam could only be a good omen.

♦

John lay across the lumpy twin sized mattress in the bedroom of his hot and stuffy apartment, rifling through the lined pages of the thick ledger he took from Hayward. His original plan was to only take a quick glance over the book before heading out to meet Sam, but he soon found himself studying its contents intently. Tucked between the various pages strewn with scribbled notations, were several dated betting slips with names, numbers and dollar amounts written on them. John immersed himself in the notes, trying to decipher the inner workings of Woody's operation in detail.

Hayward's girl had been right. Woody was bringing in a nice chunk of green putting up bank for various numbers bets while getting a piece of everybody's action this side of Harlem. A few names like Suede and Black Barry popped up numerous times on several pages. From what John could make out, it seemed as if Woody and his crew were also extorting them for some serious bank. He cracked a smile, as the wheels of his mind begin to turn on all cylinders. This ledger was going to turn out to be more important than he could have ever imagined.

While he studied the ledger, time had quickly passed by. Before he knew it, the sun had gone down and his room became dimly illuminated by the light from the street lamps that filtered through his makeshift drapes.

"Damn, I was supposed to meet Sam at the park," he thought to himself.

He knew that Sam would be worried about him, but what he didn't know was how his hotheaded brother would react. Would Sam head back to their apartment, or would he go over to Woody's bar to check on him? His stomach churned, and made a grumbling sound while he thought. He hadn't eaten since he had breakfast with Bilal earlier that morning.

John securely tucked the ledger in his jacket pocket, before heading out of the apartment. He decided to get a bite to eat at the corner store, and then wait at the apartment for another hour or so. If Sam didn't show up by then, he would head back over to Woody's. Even though he didn't want to go back to the bar today, he knew if Sam had headed over there by himself, there was a good chance that some shit could go down.

After buying some grub, he sat on a shoddy milk crate leaning up against the store. He chewed his food slowly, savoring each bite of the hot roast beef sandwich and the bag of chips he had bought only seconds earlier. The city that never sleeps had slowed to a snail's pace, as the shops closed and the people that were out on the streets began to dissipate as darkness set in. The atmosphere was unusually calm and serene for this part of town.

He took a bite out of his sandwich, just as two fine females walked past him strutting seductively.

One of the girl's eyes met his for a brief moment, before she shyly looked away. The scent of sweet perfume accompanied the female. Her eyes were pretty and brown, which reminded him of his girlfriend Michelle from back home. He purposely hadn't thought about her in so long. The days since he came up here had turned to weeks, and now it was almost a year since they last spoke. Until that very moment, he hadn't realized how much he missed her.

The calmness that arrived when the darkness set in was broken by the sound of tires screeching against the pavement, as Jimmy pulled the limo to an abrupt halt in front of *The Royal Ballroom*. He let it idle, as Woody and his muscle tucked their guns in their beltlines and slowly exited the vehicle. John calmly watched on from across the street.

Woody was sitting in the back of the limousine with three of his armed henchmen. He had been driving around for the past two hours, intensely surveying the people walking down the street. He was still fuming inside over the fact that Hayward had been parading out in the open earlier, and nobody had grabbed his ass. He made a point to put the word out on the streets hours ago, and still somebody had fucked up. Either that or somebody on this side of town was helping Hayward hide out. In any case, Woody was determined to get some answers soon.

"Incompetent imbeciles," Woody thought out loud.

After wasting away two hours, he reluctantly decided to head over to see an eccentric hustler and rival of his named, Herbert. Herbert was already waiting for them outside as they exited the limo. He was a pudgy little Black man, with every type of sense you could think of having...except a sense of fashion. But, he had the savvy and wit needed to run a successful operation of his own. Next to Woody, he was seeing the most green in Harlem. If anybody knew what was going down on this side of town, it would be him.

It was more than half way into the spring and Herbert was still wearing a green turtleneck shirt, with light blue polyester pants. Woody was very fashion conscious, so when he saw Herbert standing there ostentatiously looking like a spectacle, he wanted to laugh out hysterically. But, anger had completely engulfed him, and he couldn't will himself to even crack a smile.

Herbert carefully observed his demeanor, immediately realizing that this was not your typical social call. Normally, this place would be jammed with pimps, whores and the neighborhood's hustlers. Tonight was different though. Herbert made sure most of his crew was assembled inside his small establishment, so he confidently stood out in the open without fear. He knew that anger could drive a man to do some crazy things, but he also knew that Woody wasn't stupid. In any case, he still had to show him the respect he deserved.

Herbert was actually very happy to see the current misfortune Woody was experiencing with Hayward's disappearance. Both of them were seeing money in their respective part of town, but Woody had the advantage of being backed by the Italians. This afforded him some opportunities and protection that Herbert couldn't benefit from, which resulted in a slight degree of envy.

"Woody, how you doing baby?" Herbert asked cheerfully.

"I'm good, baby. By the looks of it, not as good as you," Woody responded emotionless.

"So, what's going on? Any word on your man Hayward?"

"Good question. That's what I'm here for. Have you seen him?"

"Nah, man. If I had seen him, you know I would've reached out to you already. Why do you ask?"

Woody frowned his face up in disbelief. "Somebody told me that they seen Hayward's ass out here earlier. So, the way I see it, somebody lying."

Herbert grinned slightly as he looked at Woody's henchmen, who all seemed agitated and ready to fire their pieces on command. He spit a thin spray of yellow phlegm through the gap between his upper row of teeth onto the sidewalk, before turning to face Woody.

"You must be losing your fucking mind Woody," Herbert said disgustedly as he shot an evil glare at him. "I fucking called you motherfucker, and offered my help when I heard about your man Melvin getting gunned down. Not vise-versa. And this is the type of thanks I get? You come to my house with a couple of petty goons trying to intimidate me?"

Woody wanted to reach out and smack the living daylights out of his ass, but he knew he was right. He had been operating off of emotions, and he was letting his imagination and wild thoughts get the best of him. He knew that he was losing his self-control, and desperately needed to regain his composure.

"I'm sorry. Shit's just fucked up right now, my man. Melvins' dead and Haywards' missing. I've been going crazy over this shit, man. And then that country dude came and told me that he seen Hayward earlier today on 145th street. Man—"

"Country dude? Who you talking about, that nigga they call Country?" Herbert asked in an astonished tone.

"He said his name was John. Tall lanky dude from the south," Woody replied.

"Yep, that's Country ahiit. That motherfucker was around here asking about you earlier today, but he wasn't with no Hayward. As a matter of fact, he was looking all spiffy and shined up today. Even had some bankroll. Which was kinda odd and shit," Herbert said as he paused to spit another stream of yellow phlegm onto the sidewalk.

"Normally he's dirty and greasy as a motherfucker. But, not today though. I asked that nigga where he got his new digs, and he said his number hit."

"That motherfucker came to see me looking to collect some money from the numbers. He said Hayward sent him to me," Woody responded coldly, as his mind began to race.

"That's some funny shit. Well in any case, it looks like you've found your liar and possibly your killer."

"When I see the nigga again, I'm a get me some motherfuckin' get back. I'm a cut that faggot's heart out and feed it to him."

Herbert gestured towards a modest looking apartment building diagonally across from where he was standing and said, "Well, Country lives right across the street, in apartment 2B on the second floor. But, I don't see the piece of shit car that he drives. He usually parks it right over there."

"That's alright, we'll wait inside for him."

John was still diagonally across the street from *The Royal Ballroom*, hidden in the shadows of the store's awning. He had been quietly observing the whole spectacle that was taking place in front of him, since Woody exited the car with a couple of his oversized goons following closely behind him. He nervously watched on as they walked up to Herbert, who was already standing outside. As he observed Woody and Herbert's animated discussion, he slowly took his piece out of the waistband of his pants, and concealed it in the sleeve of his jacket. A strange feeling of anxiety rushed over him as he saw Herbert point his pudgy index finger towards his apartment building.

He held the barrel of the pistol in the sweaty palm of his right hand, as he watched Woody and his killers head across the street and draw their guns. Traffic slowed as they made their way towards his building, impeding the paths of the oncoming cars. His throat became dry and his heart began to beat uncontrollably as they got to his side of the street, standing less than fifty feet away from him. John let the cold steel of the gun's handle slide down into the palm of his hand, as he gripped it tightly and placed his shaky index finger on the trigger. Slowly stepping out from underneath the awning with his gun in hand, he was no longer concealed by darkness.

A young petite female pedestrian was headed right towards the front door of the corner store, until she saw John standing suspiciously on the sidewalk. Noticing his gun, she frantically quickened her pace in anticipation of the mayhem that was about to take place.

The anxiety was overwhelming, but his heart rate settled as he prepared to go to war. Like clockwork, John's mind quickly began formulating a plan of attack. As he stood on the sidewalk, the headlights of a passing car pierced through the darkness and shined on the polished barrel of his black .45.

Driven by anger and emotional instability, Woody quickly led his gang towards John's apartment building without even looking towards his direction. A hobo was sitting on a cement stoop in front of the entrance to the apartment building. He saw the men approaching, and came out of his drunken stupor just as Woody pulled his .38 out of his pants line and motioned him to move out of the way. The toothless drunken old man quickly obliged, quietly slipping into the shadows as Woody and his men stormed into the old building.

John tightened his grip on the gun, preparing to launch a barrage of bullets at the killers in his midst. Sweat slicked his dark complexioned face, as he stood close by watching Woody and his gang aggressively entering the building. He thought about following them into the lobby and ambushing them. The element of surprise was on his side, but he couldn't anticipate how Herbert and his squad of killers assembled across the street would respond to his attack.

After pondering the thought for a few seconds, his eyes surveyed the block, before he determined his next move. He tucked his gun away slowly, seizing the opportunity to quietly walk off in the opposite direction. Cloaked in darkness, he disappeared down a side street. When he reached the corner, he flagged down a yellow cab. "135th and Lenox," he said to the driver, as he settled down on the cab's back seat. He was headed over to Woody's bar.

The building's decaying lobby was dimly lit by a flickering light bulb controlled by a metal chain, which intrusively hung down from the middle of the ceiling. The men quickly ran up the old wooden staircase to the second floor landing, with their guns drawn. The lead paint on the light green walls was badly chipping, exposing a dingy white layer of plaster that existed beneath. The unmistakable smell of old urine filled the air. Apartment 2B was located in the middle of the hallway.

Woody didn't hesitate as he approached the apartment, kicking in the shoddy plywood door with all his might. The door easily flew off the hinges, slamming into the apartment's plaster wall. The small one bedroom apartment was mostly empty, except for a lumpy bed, a ragged couch and an upholstered gray loveseat filled with rips and holes that sat in the middle of the living room floor. Two gray sheets hung from the blind-less windows in the bedroom, apparently being used as makeshift drapes. The men quickly spread out searching the small apartment, but uncovered nothing. Nobody was there.

"Damn, it stinks in here," Woody said, while he stood in the living room shaking his head in disgust.

"Yeah, these motherfuckers is slobs," one of the men said in concurrence.

"Hot as hell in here too," Woody said as he wiped some sweat off of his brow. "Go see what they got to drink in that fridge, Dee."

Dee walked into the small eat-in kitchen, and gave it a quick glance. Roaches feasted on the rancid food that was stuck to the unwashed dishes that were stacked foot high in the sink. Dee frowned up his face as he walked over to the fridge, grabbed the metal handle and swung it open aggressively.

"Holy shit," Dee yelled, as he stared into the steel box with a scowl of disgust on his face.

"What's up, Dee?" Woody asked in a concerned manner.

"Nothin'…nothing, shit just stinks in here. Smells like someone died in here," Dee responded.

The lumpy sofa cushion felt uncomfortable under Woody's weight. Instinctively, he lifted up the cushion, exposing a bloodied paper bag. As Woody examined its contents, one hot tear of anger slowly ran down the left side of his face, and his stomach began to churn. He held a blood stained gold chain and watch in his hand. Woody had given Hayward the gold engraved watch a couple of months back at his birthday party.

His voice cracked as he spoke to Dee, in an angry and stern fashion. "Go over to Herbert's and call the fuckin' bar. If that country motherfucker is still there, tell them to keep him there. If he's not there, tell them to find his ass!" Woody yelled out.

"Then what, Wood? You want them to kill him?" Dee asked.

"No, just tell them to hold his ass there. After I'm finished with his ass, that motherfucker will wish they had killed him," Woody said coldly.

CHAPTER 5

Hours had passed since Woody put the word out on the street for all of his henchmen to keep an eye out for the tall dark skinned son of a bitch that had murdered Hayward and Melvin. The last twenty-four hours had left him on edge, and he couldn't wait to cross paths with that country motherfucker and put some closure to this little situation before it got even further out of hand. There was a price on John's head that he would willingly payout to anyone who brought him in alive.

It was Sunday night, and *The Paradise Pool Room* on 134th street was filled with working class Blacks and street hustlers. From the outside, this hole in the wall nightspot looked like a seedy venue. But, the owner Clyde had done a good job decorating the interior nicely with a cherry wood bar, a modest sized dance floor and four pool tables. Mirrors adorned the walls, creating a club like atmosphere for the people that sat about at the tables that were positioned along the outer edges of the room.

The liquor was flowing, and so was the conversation, as the pool sharks displayed their skills in high stake games. Onlookers bet amongst themselves, flashing their bankrolls and downing whiskey like water, as the sound of clicking pool balls echoed throughout the lounge.

Sam entered the smoke filled room, quickly scanned over the patrons and then headed directly to the bar. Sharply fitted in an Italian tailored suit, he was definitely dressed for the occasion, but he still stuck out amongst the crowd. Clyde immediately noticed Sam as he made way over to the bar and slid the bartender a fifty for a bottle of Jack Daniels. He wasn't really a drinker, but he could feel the eyes throughout the room staring at him, and he wanted them to know he was holding some bankroll. Clyde knew the face of every hustler uptown. His photographic memory and uncanny ability to quickly scan a crowd and notice someone out of place, was his biggest asset. Moving swiftly through the crowd, he slid in behind Sam just as he made his way to one of the pool tables.

Link Johnson, was a contract killer who was so respected that even the Italians paid him to conduct hits. He was also a fierce pool player who rarely lost a game. Johnson was peering at the three balls left on the table, trying to figure out his next shot. Sam glanced around the table at the onlookers whose faces seemed to express doubt. It was a tough shot, which even the most skillful pool player would struggle to make. Johnson blinked his eyes to focus better, and cracked a slight smile as he chalked up his cue. Without hesitation, he leaned over and quickly stroked out his shot, banking the ball crisply and directly into the corner pocket.

"Fuck!" Little Jimmy yelled out, as the ball sank into the pocket. He was playing Johnson, and had just lost one thousand dollars.

"Pay up motherfucker," Johnson said coldly, as he took a sip from the glass of bourbon the bartender had just handed him.

Little Jimmy threw ten crisp one hundred dollar bills onto the table, which Johnson quickly snatched up. Smiling, his grin came across even cockier as he said, "Can't nobody fuck with me on the pool table!"

Sam, who was now standing directly across the table from Johnson, snarled and said, "Your pool game ain't worth shit!"

Everyone in the pool hall seemed to stop what they were doing at that very moment. Clyde, who was in an earshot of Sam, knew for certain at that moment that he couldn't be from New York. Anybody who was somebody knew that Link Johnson would drop a motherfucker for stepping on his shoes, let alone disrespecting him. Sam coolly swigged some Jack Daniels as Johnson walked over to him. His cold eyes glared directly into Sam's face as he began speaking.

"You got a lot of balls on you calling me out motherfucker."

"I call it as I see it...I mean your game's decent, but let's not get carried away and shit."

"Damn, you a little cocky sonofabitch," Johnson said as he cracked a sinister smile. He pulled out a shiny black .38 from his back pocket and placed it on the side of the pool table. "Talk is cheap though. Talking done got a lot of motherfuckers around here killed."

Sam laughed as he took another swig from his bottle. "I guess it's a good thing I ain't from around here then," he said as he pulled twenty crisp one hundred dollar bills from his pocket and placed them on the table.

"Where I'm from, actions speak a whole lot louder than words, nigga."

The hush that had just existed over the crowd quickly dissipated, replaced by whispering and people conversing about potential bets. Everyone's facial expression was dumbstruck, as they wondered who the young kid was that had the audacity to challenge Johnson, and whether or not his game was as good as his mouth was.

Johnson pulled a wad of money out of his pocket and placed it in the middle of the pool table. It was easily four or five thousand dollars. He chewed slowly on the toothpick he had in his mouth, before looking directly at Sam and grinning.

"If you win, all that shit right there is yours. But, when I win, you leave this motherfuckin' pool hall the same way you came into this world nigga...no cash and buck naked!"

The crowd of onlookers laughed out loud hysterically at the thought of Sam leaving the pool hall with his tail between his legs. Undaunted, Sam nodded his head accepting the bet. He moved his money off of the table so they could get down to business, and Johnson did the same. His eyes were big, and his heart fluttered in anticipation of receiving his winnings.

He walked over to a rack that was against the wall and chose a stick for himself. Unlike most pool players, Sam never had a stick of his own to use when he hustled people out of their money in the south. He was too broke for that. So, he was accustomed to playing with any old stick. Little

Jimmy racked up the balls, smiling at Link as he prepared the table. "I got a hundred on the kid."

"Then your monkey ass just lost another hundred," Johnson snarled back in response.

Sam chalked up his cue as he looked over the table. He motioned to Johnson, giving him the go ahead to break, but he waved him off. "You break young blood."

Sam took a deep breath, leaned over and calmly made his break shot, delivering a glancing blow that left the pack of balls nearly intact. The white cue ball drifted off on its own, ending up at the far end of the table. It was exactly as he planned it. Sam figured that there wasn't much for Johnson to work with. He backed away from the table and cracked a sarcastic smile. Undaunted, Johnson took his toothpick out of his mouth and placed it on the side of the table, as he peered at the balls.

"I don't know where you from young blood, but this how we play in Harlem," Johnson said, pausing as he lined up his shot. "Fifteen in corner pocket!"

His eyes quickly studied the table, as his arm and wrist moved in another fluid motion.

"Six in the corner." The cue ball guided the six swiftly into the corner pocket. Johnson pranced around the table in a cocky fashion, as he sized up his next shot.

"Where you from young blood?"

"South Carolina."

"Well, I always heard that you southern motherfuckers wasn't too bright," Johnson said, laughing out loud. The onlookers laughed amongst themselves, as Sam looked on with a cold facial expression.

Clyde backed away from the table, calmly walking through the crowd to his office, which was located on the right side of the bar. His instincts never lead him astray, and when he heard the young cocky sonofabitch at the pool table mention South Carolina, a light bulb went off in his head. He knew that Woody and his boys were looking for a guy from the south that had murdered Hayward and Melvin. He closed his office door and grabbed the phone, calling over to Woody's bar. He reached Jive Talk, who told him to call Herbert, because Woody had headed over there earlier.

Clyde called over to *The Royal Ballroom*, and was placed on hold as they sent someone to the apartment house across the street to get Woody. Clyde was growing impatient listening to dead air on the other side of the line. He was about to hang up, just as someone picked up and began speaking.

"What's happenin? This is Woody."

"Woody, long time no see baby. It's Clyde."

"What's up, Clyde?"

"I'm over at my pool hall, and I think there's a motherfucker here that you might want to take a close look at?"

"Why you say that?"

"Southern, tall...he's not dark skinned, but he's holding a hell of a lot of green."

Woody's insides became hot with anger. "Keep that motherfucker there. I'll be over in a minute!"

The Royal Ballroom was only a few blocks away. Clyde walked out of his office and headed back towards the table that Sam and Johnson were playing at. Johnson was still putting on an exhibition, displaying skills that the seasoned pool sharks that were present didn't even know he had.

"Twelve in the side pocket," Johnson yelled as he curled his bejeweled fingers around his cue stick and banked the cue ball off of the side of the table effectively sinking the shot.

"I'm a bad, bad man!" Johnson yelled out slyly for all those in the poolroom to hear.

By now, Sam had accepted the fact that he wasn't going to beat him at billiards. His mind had raced ahead, as he tried to figure out how he was going to make it out of the poolroom with his money, as well as Johnson's. The place was tight, and Johnson seemed to be respected amongst the clientele. Sam knew it wasn't going to be easy, but his hunger and desire for money was giving him unwarranted confidence.

Johnson was showboating around the table, when Clyde approached him and whispered something into his ear. He nodded in acknowledgment, and then he sharpened his cue stick slowly.

"Make that a double shot," Johnson said to Clyde, who was on his way to the bar. About five minutes passed, as he waited patiently for Clyde to return with his drink. Once he got it, he quickly gulped down every drop of brown liquid that was in the shot glass.

"Yeah!" He yelled out as the liquor burnt his throat, and rushed straight to his head. He looked over the table, steadied his cue stick and lined up his shot.

"Three ball in the corner pocket," he yelled out as he thrust his stick forward. The cue ball knocked into the three, sending it careening against the side of table, missing the corner pocket. Sam smiled, realizing that he finally had his shot to take control of the game. He looked over the table, trying to plot out his next move.

Sam was absorbed by his thoughts, concentrating completely on the game. As he leaned over to prepare to take his shot, he instinctively noticed two suspicious characters standing amongst the crowd. He eyed the exit, and saw two more henchmen that hadn't been there earlier. Even with the lights dimmed, Sam visibly noticed the bulges from their pieces through their overcoats. He scanned the room again, and noticed that the crowd was slowly starting to dissipate. He spotted the bloodthirsty eyes of two more killers trying to slowly move through the room unnoticed. He knew that they were getting in position to make their move on him shortly.

Sam pretended to be unaware of what was going on in his surroundings. Johnson had slipped in behind him and his .38 was no longer resting on the side of the pool table. Sam gripped his cue stick as he leaned in to eye his shot.

"Three in the corner pocket," Sam yelled out.

In one swift motion he pivoted his body and swung his cue stick backwards with full force. It grotesquely smashed into the bridge of Johnson's nose, breaking in half on impact. Blood sprayed into the air as he let out a loud scream of agony and fell to the floor holding his face.

Immediately, shots rang out loudly, shattering the mirrors that had beautifully adorned the walls. The killers were shooting aimlessly, and innocent bystanders were getting caught in the crossfire as they ran wildly for the exit. Sam dived behind the pool table as bullets flew through the air, ripping through the green felt that lined the tabletop. With his back pressed up against the table, he fumbled with his pistol, as he tried to grab it out of his waistline.

He struggled to gain his composure as shattered glass rained down all around him. Bodies were getting trampled, and confusion and fear filled the air. Sam peeked his head out from the side of the pool table, attempting to locate his enemies amidst the carnage. A bullet whizzed past his head, barely missing him. He jumped backwards, and planted his back against the table again. He was clutching his piece in his right hand, but he didn't see many options that would allow him to make it to the exit door.

"He's over here Woody! I got the motherfucker pinned behind the pool table on the right!" One of Woody's henchman yelled out.

"Keep that motherfucker pinned! I want bullets from my gun to kill that motherfucker," Woody yelled out. His deep voice carried over the noise that was prevalent throughout the club.

"Concentrate nigga...fuckin' concentrate," Sam whispered to himself.

He knew time was running out for him. He was a sitting duck behind the pool table, and his enemies had so many different directions they could attack him from. Sam reached down and picked a small piece of glass up from the floor. The jagged edges of the broken mirror cut through the tip of his finger, but his adrenaline was running too wildly for him to feel any pain. His right hand shook involuntarily as he held the mirror out to his side, moving it around until he spotted one of the killers walking towards him in a crouching stance. He was less than ten feet away from Sam, and quickly closing the gap between them.

Without hesitation Sam quickly peeked around the table while squeezing the trigger of his .45. The bullets sailed swiftly through the air, ripping into the killer's rib cage exploding forcefully through his back. As the killer's body crumpled to the floor, another henchman ran up shooting wildly into the air. Sam fell into a crouching position as the bullets flew past him. He aimed his gun at the henchman's leg, and squeezed once. Meat and bone fragments from his knee burst into the air, as his legs buckled from beneath him and he yelled out in a fit of agony.

Sam hurriedly crawled back behind the pool table. The front door was now open, and the bystanders who had been hiding to avoid the bullets that were flying through the air, were now running out of the pool hall for dear life. Sam spotted six more of Woody's men making their way towards him and he only had two bullets left in his gun.

"You's a dead motherfucker!" Woody yelled out. His voice emanated from Sam's left. He didn't know how many men were approaching from that direction. Johnson had mysteriously disappeared during the shootout, and the killers Sam had blasted weren't close enough for him to grab one of their weapons. Crawling over to them would put him directly in harm's way. He took a deep breath and clutched his piece tightly in the palm of his hand.

"Come and get me motherfuckers," he yelled out confidently.

"We coming motherfucker," Woody said in his deep baritone voice. "You about to meet your motherfuckin' maker."

Bullets rang out hitting the pool table that Sam was crouched behind. Upon impact, shards of wood rained through the air. Sam prepared for the inevitable, but then a dead calm went over the room, as each second that passed seemed to be an eternity. The lounge was virtually empty except for Woody and his killers, the innocent bystanders who were too badly injured to get out of the club and Sam. Sweat flowed down his forehead as he got ready to make his move.

"WhatamIawoodorwhat?" The words were barely out of Curtis's mouth, before the sound of his shotgun burst out loudly, echoing throughout the hall. The shell slammed into the head of one of the henchman, blowing bloody brain matter out of his skull. Woody's men turned to face the door, just as Sam jumped to his feet, adrenalin rushing through his body like a madman. He squeezed his trigger, sending a bullet at one of the henchman that was standing five feet away from him. The shot ripped through the side of his cheek, tearing away the right side of his face.

"Boom!" From a kneeling position, Curtis blasted his shotgun again, sending one of the killer's bodies flying backwards through the air, his intestines grossly splattering one of the pool tables.

Woody and his killers were frightened and confused now. They fired their guns in the air aimlessly, unable to spot their targets. Doc was kneeling down walking through the poolroom unnoticed, using his marksmanship skills to take out the henchman one by one. He easily blended into the shadows, as he quietly crept up on the unsuspecting killers. Curtis had tossed his shotgun, and was now positioned behind the bar, letting off shots from a rusty .38 he found on the floor.

Screams of pain and agony filled the air, as more and more of the hired guns were sent to meet their maker. Realizing that he was outgunned, Woody began crawling towards the door quickly. The sound of gunfire echoed behind him, as he quietly slivered on the floor within a couple of feet of the front door. Now kneeling, he was just about to stand up and run out the door, when he felt the piece of cold steel pressed up against his forehead.

"Where you going? The party's just getting started," Sam asked, with a sarcastic grin on his face.

"Look man, I got two hundred long at my pad man. I can give you — " Sam interrupted him as he pleaded for his life.

"Shh...Shh..." Sam said, holding his pointer finger to his mouth. "You're ruining this shit for me man. I mean, they told me you were like Al Capone or some shit, and you here crying like a little bitch."

"Please...just don't — "

"Stand the fuck up, nigga!"

Woody stood up, and Sam held his .45 pressed flush against the back of his temple. With his other hand, he reached in Woody's pant's pocket and removed a knot of cash.

"Curt," Sam yelled.

"Yeah," Curtis responded from behind the bar.

"Doc," Sam yelled.

"Right here," Doc said as he stood up.

"Let's get the fuck outta here," Sam said, after confirming that they were both alive and well.

Sam kicked open the front door, and tapped Woody on the back of his head with the revolver, motioning him to go out of the pool hall. Curt watched their backs, and Doc scanned the streets as they all walked out onto the sidewalk. There were still some people outside who had been in the poolroom, nosily waiting around to see the outcome of the bloodbath that was taking place inside. Sam was happy to have an audience, as he stood on the sidewalk with his gun to Woody's neck.

"So, this is the baddest motherfucker in Harlem, huh?" Sam yelled loudly to no one in particular.

The onlookers stared on, hiding behind cars and across the street out of harm's way.

"Well, there's some new motherfuckers in town niggas!" Sam yelled, as he squeezed down on his trigger.

The last bullet in his gun entered the right side of Woody's neck, and exited through the left, sending pieces of his esophagus sailing through the air as his limp body crumpled to the sidewalk. A woman kneeling behind a car parked across the street gasped in disbelief.

"Fix your fuckin' face," Sam said coldly, as he walked with Curtis and hopped into Doc's old Plymouth that was parked in front of a fire hydrant next to the poolroom. Doc started it up, and the muffler roared loudly. As he revved the engine, the car backfired startling those on the street even further, causing them to duck for cover. Doc put the car in gear, slowly pulling off down the street, leaving a trail of thick white smoke behind his car.

"Just like old times," Doc said as he looked over at Sam who was riding shotgun.

"Yeah, just like old times. You two was late as usual," Sam responded sarcastically.

"Better late than never, right?" Doc said.

"You got that right," Sam responded, while reaching out and slapping Doc five. "Better late than never."

CHAPTER 6

John had stood in the shadows, quietly watching Woody's bar from across the street. After waiting a while, and seeing no sign of Sam, he headed towards the Wilson's pad over on 113th. Sam and Doc were still awake, sitting on the couch talking about the shootout they had just participated in when he arrived. Curtis was out cold on the bed in the back room snoring loudly.

Sam and Doc replayed every intricate detail of the gunfight for John, making sure they harped over the fact that he missed all of the action. Sam animatedly acted out the entire pool hall scene, using the couch and kitchen table as props. He hopped back and forth, rolling on the floor and making gun sounds with his mouth for further emphasis. Every couple of sentences or so, Doc would chime in adding his own little comments on the whole event. John continued listening on, barely believing that in his brief absence, so much had transpired. But nonetheless, he was happy that everyone was alive and well. He shared his story with Doc and Sam, explaining why he was unable to make it to the park. After a few hours of chatting and catching up on old times, they all dosed off to sleep.

When the sun's bright rays began to shine through the dingy cracked glass of the living room window, Curtis staggered into the room, looking like he could use about eight more hours of rest. His eyes were bloodshot red, and he had crusty dried up drool on one of his cheeks. He nudged John a couple of times, waking him up just as he collapsed onto the raggedy couch next to him.

"Hot diggety dang! Da whole damn gang done back toget," Curtis said enthusiastically. The commotion woke Doc and Sam up, as he continued talking. "Man Johnny, you shoulda seen did us up in deer man. We was pluckin' them motherfuckers away like ducks. And then that faggot fuckin' begdid Sam like a girl for his life."

Sam smiled on excitedly. John looked at the excitement on his brother's face. He had the same sickening glint in his eyes that existed after he killed Hayward...after he knifed his girlfriend to death. As they began to slap each other five, replaying the events from last night over again, John stood up off of the couch and interrupted them.

"Let me play devil's advocate here, or just be straight up with you Skeet. You motherfuckers got lucky last night. Point blank, that shit was fuckin' luck. Niggas underestimated yawl, so niggas is dead. But, that shit won't happen again, trust me."

"Nah, Johnny those motherfuckers couldn't fuck with us. When Doc and Curtis came through the door—"

"They surprised the hell out of them. But, the element of surprise is now gone. In less than a heartbeat, we went from being some backward ass country motherfuckers, to some organized hit men," John said, pausing as he looked around the room studying their faces. "Listen, do yawl really believe that anybody thinks that four motherfuckers is responsible for taking out Woody's crew?"

He looked at their faces, which were all expressionless. Sam shrugged his shoulders, but didn't comment. John could tell they all got his point.

"All I'm saying is that if anybody knew it was only four of us, we'd all be dead now," John said.

"So, what do you suggest," Doc asked, looking directly at John. It was just like old times. Whenever their backs were up against the wall, they turned to John for direction. His intelligence demanded respect. His decision making skills were unquestionable.

"It's according to what everybody in this room agrees to. I mean, we can count our blessings, thank god that we all made it through the past twenty four hours alive, and head out of town." John said.

"Or?" Sam asked.

John cracked a smile, looking around the room again before responding. "Or, we can capitalize off of this shit, and start making some real money."

"*WhatamIawoodorwhat?*" Curtis yelled out, slapping John on his back excitedly. "We fittin' to make some cash!"

"So, what's your plan Johnny? I know you always got a plan," Doc asked inquisitively.

"We need bodies," John said as he sat down on the arm of the couch.

"You want me to see if we can recruit some of Woody's old gang?" Doc asked.

"That's an option, but I would prefer to bring some more boys up from the south," John said, turning his body towards Doc. "You feel like taking a ride down there?"

"I don't mind, but if I head down there, you gon' have one less body," Doc said, with a concerned look on his face.

"That's true. Plus, how many niggas you gonna be able to fit in that car anyway? With your luck, that shit'll break down somewhere and all yawl motherfuckers'll get lynched and shit," John said sarcastically, letting out a huge laugh.

"Fuck you Johnny!" Doc responded.

"Why don't you take a couple of g's over to Western Union and wire it down to Lazy Eyed Cleon, Tyrone Parks, and Stink Harris," John said, pausing as he took a knot of twenties out of his pocket and threw it to Doc. "Oh yeah, and anybody else that wanna come up here and make some green."

"Shiiittt!!! I'll get Stink to pack as many of them motherfuckers as they can fit into one of them piece of shit Greyhounds, and bring em up here." Everybody laughed out loud again.

Doc stood up, looked over to John and said, "Seriously, Johnny...I mean all jokes aside nigga, we need some new rides. My piece of shit Plymouth is on its last legs nigga."

Everybody laughed out loud again. Sam got up off the couch, now fully awake.

"So, what are we gonna do while those motherfuckers head up here? We just gonna sit around and wait?" Sam asked.

"Nah. You know what they say, time waits for no one," John looked around, cracking a wide smile as he scanned everyone's face again. "Our motherfuckin' time is now."

Around the same time on the other side of Harlem, little nine year-old Mookie Dunbar and his friend Chris had just started playing hide and seek. Mookie ran carelessly through the weeds, shattered glass and rocks that were strewn across the dirt lot that sat between two dilapidated buildings where he played often. He was playing hide and seek with a couple of his friends, as he did most mornings, frantically running around looking for the ideal hiding place.

"Eight Mississippi, nine Mississippi," he mouthed to himself, trying to keep track of how much time he had left to hide. His friend Chris was much faster than him, so he knew he had to find a hiding space quick. As he ran through the lot, he saw an old blue Impala parked by the curb. The beat up jalopy immediately stuck out to him. They typically played "that's my car" as they sat on the stoop in front of their building or played in this lot, and he never noticed this raggedy car before. Not that he would have picked it as his ride, but it stuck out to him, and looked like the perfect hiding place.

"Chris will never find me if I hide under there," he thought to himself as he approached the unoccupied car.

Slowly he walked to the car, cautiously looking around to make sure he was unnoticed. As he bent down by the rear of the car, he smelled a horrible stench that emanated from the rusty trunk. The scent was so overwhelming that he still smelled the odor after tightly squeezing his thumb and pointer finger over his nose.

"You're it," Chris yelled, as he crept up behind Mookie, and tapped him on the shoulder. Caught off guard, Mookie jumped backwards awkwardly.

"Shit, you scared the hell outta me!" Mookie yelled.

"What the hell is that smell? You farted?" Chris asked, as he frowned up his face.

"Nah, that's your momma's drawers," Mookie responded sarcastically.

"Fuck you, Mook. I'm serious. What the hell is that shit?"

"I don't know, but it sure does stink."

A latchkey kid since he was seven, Chris never went anywhere without a set of keys in his pocket. He pulled a brass key ring out of his pocket, and started trying one of the keys on the lock. Working the key from side to side, he tried his best to force it into the lock, but it didn't fit. He examined his key ring until he came across a smaller key that looked like a better fit. Just as he was about to try it in the lock, Mookie noticed a police cruiser slowly driving down the street.

"Run, it's the pigs!" Mookie yelled, as he ran at top speed through the lot. Chris frantically followed behind him.

Officer Ward pulled up next to the car the boys had been standing by. He was parked down the block eating a jelly donut in his squad car, when he noticed the two adolescents fiddling with the car's trunk. He didn't chase after the kids, deciding to first check and see if any damage was done to the car. As he approached the car, he noticed the presence of several large flies, as his nostrils inhaled the very familiar stench of death.

Ward slowly walked to his squad car, and made a call to the stationhouse on his radio. He asked the dispatcher to run the car's plate "X56-55y", which came back as being reported stolen just the night before. He paused momentarily to gain his composure, before he reluctantly walked back over to the car and jimmied the trunk. The old lock easily gave way as he applied pressure.

As the trunk popped open, his suspicions of foul play were immediately confirmed. Maggots had already begun to go to work on the two bodies, one male and one female, which were stuffed into the trunk. Ward gagged, as he struggled not to upchuck the breakfast he had just downed. As he gained his composure, he looked over the bodies once again, immediately recognizing the body of the male as the notorious Hayward Jones. The hustler had finally been found, a day after his boss was gunned down in cold blood.

In Staten Island, another conversation was taking place regarding Woody's death. Francis "Fat Frankie" Dileonardo was puffing on a fat Cuban cigar, leaning back in a leather recliner, thumbing through the day's *New York Post*. As he leaned backwards, his white t-shirt rose up above his belly button revealing hundreds of stretch marks that crisscrossed his flabby stomach like dissecting train tracks. With a massive frame that easily exceeded four hundred pounds, Frankie could usually be found sitting down. Asthma and various complications resulting from his excessive weight caused him to frequently experience bouts with shortness of breath when he walked.

After rereading the short paragraph on page 23 titled, *Harlem Numbers Kingpin Gunned Down*, he tossed the paper down on a glass table next to his chair, and took a big bite out of a roll saturated with cream cheese and grape jelly.

His lieutenant, Luciano DelBracio sat across from him, on one of the loveseats that he had in his spacious office. Luci, which was the sobriquet his friends addressed him by, was Frank's most loyal worker and consigliere. He called Fat Frankie as soon as he heard the news, and made a point to pick up the paper on his way to his house that morning. Frankie puffed on his cigar, slowly exhaling a cloud of white smoke out of his mouth. He rested his stogie in an ashtray, as he leaned forward in his seat to speak to Luci.

"You know, I really liked Woody. He was a good guy. I mean, he had decent qualities for a nigger," Frankie said, using hand gestures to emphasize his words.

"Yeah, I liked him too. But, the fuckin' world don't run on like or love," Luci responded coldly. "Now we're left in a motherfuckin' quandary here."

"How you figure Luci?"

"Well, all of the niggers knew that Woody was our guy. They're gonna be fuckin' expecting us to retaliate. Get some fuckin' retribution. You get what I'm saying?"

"Fuck them Luci. We'll just sit back and let the spooks fight it out amongst themselves, like the savages they are."

"What about the money from the numbers?"

"*Fuhgetaboutit.* A month or so ain't gonna hurt us too bad. Besides, New York State is trying to muscle its way into the numbers racket anyway, with all this fuckin' talk of a state run lottery. I just think we need to back off for a little while and see how the fuckin' balance of power shifts."

"What about fat ass Herbert? I'm sure he'd be happy to take over Woody's role."

"Nah. I never liked that eccentric sonofabitch. He's a weird mother fuck,"

"Yeah, but he has the manpower."

"Good fuckin' point. But, he lacks direction…he lacks cojones. He must be too busy dressing like a fuckin' circus clown, or else he would have taken out Woody way before the motherfuckers who did it last night."

They both laughed out loud, before Luci said, "So bottom line, you want me to stay put Frankie?"

"Stay put."

"You don't want me to do nuttin?"

"Do nuttin'…for now. The world could do with a few less spooks anyway. "

Intoxication

CHAPTER 7

The weeks and months that followed Woody's bloody murder, flew by in the blink of an eye. The whole balance of power in the Harlem landscape shifted almost overnight, as the local players scrambled to seize their share of the crumbs that Woody had left behind. Most of the scattered remnants of Woody's old crew aligned with John out of fear. Some paid him protection, while others negotiated wisely, giving him a fair stake in their numbers spots. They didn't know what that country nigga and his crew of killers were capable of.

John had been wise enough to quickly assemble a fresh batch of money hungry recruits that he helped migrate up from the south. His crew of childhood friends became his group of loyal lieutenants that he purposely made highly visible on the uptown streets. Those that didn't roll with him aligned themselves with Herbert, or a young numbers runner named Suede that started a numbers bank of his own, and was now on the come up.

John's hands now stunk, emitting the stale deathly odor that could only be described as the undeniable scent that accompanies murder. No matter how coldhearted the killer, any murderer knows that you can't wash away the blood of a man whose life you've taken. It stays with you. And it eventually consumes many. John battled within himself daily, trying to rationalize and convince himself that those whose lives he had taken were murderers themselves. But, the life of crime that he desperately tried to keep his little brother away from had become his own reality. And Sam's fragile life was spiraling out of control.

Hayward and Woody's murders had been John's initiation, resulting in more blood staining his hands. The game was becoming more and more intoxicating, as they began to delve deeper and deeper into the life of crime.

NYC's Sanitation department had done a commendable job, but dirty snow was still scattered about on the pavement, the result of winter blowing it's cold breath through Harlem only a couple of days earlier. The brutal weather had snuck up on the entire east coast, and meteorologists were predicting another two to four inches would plaster New York in the next couple of days. Still in all, the frigid conditions didn't stop a small crowd from gathering in a cramped apartment vestibule uptown, braving the cold weather.

"Would you roll the dice nigga," Black spewed out venomously as he rubbed his ashy hands together in an effort to warm them up. His tall slim body shivered from the cold. He licked his chapped white lips that were so dry, they looked as if they were seconds away from bleeding.

Sam smiled at him sarcastically, before slowly bending down and sending the white dice rolling across the tiled hallway floor.

"Seven, motherfucker," Sam yelled as he jumped up off of the floor and placed his hands in the pockets of his full-length mink coat. "Pay the fuck up!" The dice had barely stopped rolling before he celebrated, in anticipation of a good roll.

"That's three g's you owe me nigga. Pay the fuck up," Sam yelled out again, even louder than before. He pointed his finger in Black's face for further emphasis.

"Shiiit. Double or nothing, Sam. Come on, double or nothing nigga," Black responded pleadingly, as he threw a thick knot of hundreds down on the floor.

Curt was watching on intently, standing amongst the five people that were gathered around looking on. He laughed to himself, as he gazed over to Sam and said, "This motherfucker ova here dunno about you Skeet."

"Yeah, somebody shoulda told his monkey ass sumthin," Sam said, as he pulled two rubber band wrapped knots of hundreds out of his coat pocket and threw them on the cracked tile.

"Fuck you," Black responded in a harsh tone, as he frowned up his face. He shrugged his shoulders, before reaching down and grabbing the dice off of the floor. "First nigga to hit seven or eleven takes the bank."

"Whatever. Roll the dice nigga," Sam said, as he folded his arms and rested them on his chest.

Black confidently shook the dice in his hands, and blew a foggy mist on them a couple of times.

"Come on, I need you two bitches to give me a seven. Come on you no good bitches."

He let go of the dice causing them to skip lightly across the uneven floor. One of the dice landed with the number three facing straight up. The second die landed partially on a crack in the floor, with the number four visibly exposed on top.

"Seven motherfucker, seven! Give me the green," Black yelled, as he bent down to pick up his winnings. A hush quickly came over the crowd, as they waited to see Sam's reaction.

Sam's mouth frowned up in disgust, as his body became hot with anger. Driven by rage, he instinctively pulled his .45 out of his waistband and placed it against the back of Black's skull.

"What the fuck are you doing, nigga?" Black yelled out. His body tensed, and his voice noticeably cracked as he spoke. One of his boys in the crowd tried to reach towards his waistband for his pistol without being noticed, but Curt already had the drop on him.

"No, no, no," he said in his deep baritone voice, as he waived his pistol towards him.

Sam was collecting the knots of money off of the ground with one hand, as he kept the cold steel of his gun pressed to the back of Black's head with the other.

"You's a cheatin' motherfucker, huh? The fuckin' dice landed on a crack, and you gonna try to snatch up my green?" Sam asked in harsh tone.

"What the fuck you talking bout? I won that shit fair and —" He cut his sentence short, as Sam cocked back the hammer on his pistol.

"Shh...It's your money or your life, nigga. I don't respect cheaters," Sam yelled out angrily. The crowd backed away, as he rose up from the ground slowly, still clutching his pistol.

"Come on, Curt," Sam said, as he backed out of the vestibule, taking small steps towards his black

Lincoln that was double-parked on the street. Curt kept his piece trained on the crowd as he followed closely behind Sam. Cautiously he sat in the driver's seat and quickly drove off after Sam closed the passenger's door.

Sam laughed out loud as he looked at the commotion they left behind, in his rear view mirror. Easing back into his seat, he smiled feeling satisfied. Curt continued driving along, following the speed of traffic. When he felt comfortable that they were far enough away, he tucked his gun securely under the seat.

Unable to hide his emotions, Sam turned towards Curtis excitedly. He had a big grin on his face, as he said, "You see how simple these motherfuckers is, Curt?"

Curt nodded his head in agreement, but he couldn't hide his concern, which was written all over his face.

"What the hell is wrong with you?" Sam asked.

"That der nigga Black is Suede's right hand man."

Sam smiled and slammed his fist down on the dashboard, before responding.

"Do you think I give a fuck about nigga named Suede, Curt? Suede is a motherfuckin' fabric, nigga. I put holes in motherfuckin' clothes!" Sam yelled out, punching Curt in the shoulder playfully.

Curt laughed out loud. "You's is a crazy motherfucker Skeet. You's crazy!"

◆

Herbert sat behind a cluttered desk that sat in the middle of his modestly sized office, conveniently located in the back of his bar. It was decorated nicely with chairs that matched the antique mahogany desk. Banking slips and other crumpled pieces of paper were scattered aimlessly about. Apparently, his filing system was as confusing and unorganized as his colorful wardrobe.

Today, he was wearing a green blazer, blue pants with sharp creases and a white mock necked shirt. His right hand man Leroy Gates sat directly across from him, taking long pulls from a sweet tasting Cuban. The expensive Italian suit and imported loafers he wore made him look and smell like money. He sat back comfortably in a beige leather recliner, the frown lines in his forehead from mounting stress clearly visible.

"This is the third one of your number's spots that's been robbed in the past month, Herb. You're gonna have to send a message sooner or later. Preferably sooner," Leroy stated eloquently.

He was a criminal lawyer by trade, educated by the esteemed professors at NYU. Leroy benefited lovely from being a mulatto. The pale skin and curly hair he inherited from his father helped him to fit right in with society's elite. His knowledge of the street came from his fine dark skinned mother, Wilene. Wilene was a cleaning lady for the Gates family, a name synonymous with money. Robert Gates always had an undeniable craving for brown sugar, and his sloppy affair with Wilene had resulted in Leroy's birth.

Wilene stopped working for the Gates family shortly after discovering that she was pregnant. Even though she gave Leroy the last name "Gates", she never revealed his father to anyone, not even her closest friends. Robert tried his best to do the right thing, paying her considerably well for her loyalty and silence. He never had a desire to actually meet Leroy, but his monthly check arrived like clockwork until his untimely demise a few years back. Wilene had wisely banked a good portion of the money she received, which allowed Leroy to pay for his hefty college tuition.

He had been on Herbert's payroll ever since he successfully represented him in a minor assault case five years ago. Herbert respected his opinion more than anyone else that he rolled with. Leroy was intelligent and unbiased. His advice and opinions were unadulterated and uninfluenced by any outside factions. Herbert never went against his advice.

"What do you suggest Leroy? I kill that nigga over the scraps I keep at the numbers spots?" Herbert asked.

"You know, I don't make suggestions. At least not any that may have criminal implications associated with them," Leroy replied.

"Then why bring the shit up then?"

"Because Woody's gone, and the whole old school regime has changed. You represent that old school regime, Herb. Suede and that country nigga are forging the new Harlem landscape as we speak. If you don't take care of Suede now, I fear that you will soon be joining Woody."

He had Herbert's full attention now. The number spots getting robbed didn't really matter to

Herbert. The money taken was minimal, and besides, that was the spot manager's responsibility. He was more infuriated by the money that he bankrolled Suede to get established in the business that was never returned to him. This pissed him off to no end.

"So what are you saying? Stop talking in fucking riddles. Should I have Suede taken out? I gave that young motherfucker his start, now he's got me for like $20 g's."

"Who's the lesser of the two evils, Suede or country? I've always feared the unpredictable. It's easy to anticipate the next move of a foe that is predictable."

"So, I should kill that nigga Country? Country's not the one robbing my number's joints though. He don't owe me 20 g's."

"Why don't you ask Country to collect the money that Suede owes you? Give him a little off the top."

"And what's that gonna do, get me my money back? What about the robberies, should I just let that go?"

Leroy smiled, exposing his pearly white teeth as he slowly took another pull from his cigar.

"Country and Suede are very hungry, young, entrepreneurial cats. Do you think that Suede is just going to give Country your money? If that causes a street war, at least you wouldn't be directly involved."

A light bulb must have turned on in Herbert's head. A wide grin came across his face, as he picked the receiver off of his rotary phone set and quickly began dialing numbers. The phone rang momentarily, before a baritone voice on the other end said, "Hello."

"Let me speak to John," Herbert said.

"Who's this?" Doc asked inquisitively.

"Tell him it's Herbert."

"Let me see if he's available."

A brief silence came over the line while Doc passed the phone over to John, who was in the middle of counting a wad of fifties. Herbert waited patiently, before the silence was broken by John's voice.

"Well, well, well...to what do I owe this pleasure?" John asked.

"Hey John, long time no hear from baby. How you been?"

"Good, good. I can't complain. What's shaking my man?"

"I got a little business proposition for you," Herbert said.

"Speak up."

"I don't know if you heard of this motherfucker named Suede, but that fuckin' faggot owes me $20 g's."

"And you want me to collect that shit for you, huh?"

"Yeah, you got it my man. There's five thousand in it for you."

"Five thousand? Ha, ha, ha. You're really breaking the bank on this," John responded sarcastically, laughing out loud before continuing. "Listen, I don't need your five g's, but it will be my pleasure to get your money back for you. You know, we'll just consider it a favor."

"A favor?" Herbert asked in astonishment.

"Exactly. I mean, what's a little favor between friends?"

"Ha, ha, a motherfuckin' favor, huh? My man Johnny…Motherfuckin' Johnny Favors."

John looked over at Doc, stretched his lips into a sarcastic smile and pointed to the phone. Doc smiled back at him, just as he responded to Herbert.

"Johnny Favors. I like that shit. Listen, I'll take care of your little problem in the next few weeks. I have some other stuff to attend to, and then I'm on it like white on rice."

"No rush, baby. I definitely appreciate it though, my main man. Say, let's keep this little *favor* between me and you o.k?"

"No problem. I know the deal."

Satisfied, Herbert hung up the phone and cracked a sinister grin at Leroy Gates. Leroy continued puffing slowly on his cigar, as he nodded his head at Herbert.

"You're a smart motherfucker Leroy, smart as hell."

Leroy stood up from his chair, and put his trench coat on. He took one final pull from his cigar, before placing it in the marble ashtray on Herbert's desk.

"Don't try to involve or implicate me in *your* well thought out plan to destroy your enemies. I didn't have shit to do with this."

"Always the lawyer," Herbert said, before laughing aloud. This was the reason he kept Leroy on payroll. His knowledge was irreplaceable.

"Always, Herb…always," Leroy responded. He paused to shake Herbert's hand, frowning his face slightly, as a thought suddenly came over him.

"Did he ask why *you* asked *him* to collect *your*

money? I mean, he didn't want to know why *you* couldn't just get it *yourself*?"

"Nah, that backwards country nigga just said he'd do that *favor* for me...didn't even want money for it. Those country motherfuckers ain't to swift Leroy."

"Hmmm...interesting.Unpredictable indeed," Leroy muttered to himself, as he walked out of the office slowly and in deep thought.

Herbert closed the door behind him, and sat down behind his desk gloating. "One down, one to go," he coldly whispered to himself.

Across town, John sat quietly, picking up exactly where he left off counting his wad of green. Doc wanted to ask him what the phone call was all about, but he waited patiently, not wanting to break his concentration.

"Twenty-five, twenty-five fifty, twenty-six," John said out loud, before pausing midstream and looking directly at Doc, reading his facial expression. "You can talk to me Doc. I'm not gonna lose count man."

"What did that nigga want?" Doc asked.

"He wants me to collect some money from some nigga named Suede for him."

"Suede? Yeah, I heard of that nigga before. Listen Johnny, I don't trust that motherfucker, Herbert. I don't trust his fat ass as far as I can throw him. Which ain't far. What'd you tell him?"

"I told him I'd do that shit."

"Come on John, I know you don't trust that funny dressing cat? What if that nigga's setting you up?"

John ignored his questions, and began counting his money again. "Twenty-six fifty, twenty-seven hundred, twenty-seven fifty."

"John...John! Oh, you just gonna ignore me now?"

John cracked a smile as he rubber band wrapped his thick wad of fifties. "Doc, when have you ever known me to get into some trouble without a plan?"

"I know John, you's always been a thinker. But, you gotta give me your word on sumthin."

"What's that?" John asked in an annoyed tone.

"Come on, man. Just tell me yes. A second ago you was Johnny fuckin' Favors to that nigga. Can't you do me a favor too?"

John laughed out loud. "Man, you's real funny, Doc. Real funny. What's the favor?"

"Promise me that you won't do shit until I get back from Williston."

"That's it?"

"Yep, that's it. Just make me that promise."

"Damn, Doc. I never expected to see you so emotional. I never knew you cared so much," John said as he rubbed his eyes and pretended like he was crying.

Doc punched him in the arm and said, "Fuck you, Johnny." They both laughed, as John punched him back on his shoulder.

"You've got my word, Doc. I'll wait a week before I do anything."

"Thanks, Johnny," Doc said, before slapping him five. An uneasy feeling came over him as soon as he heard Herbert's voice on the other end of the line. He didn't want anything to go down before he returned from his trip, which couldn't be soon enough in his mind.

CHAPTER 8

John was always captivated by Harlem and its remarkable beauty. Sometimes he just found himself staring outside through his window, fully enthralled by the city within a city. What others took for granted, he came to appreciate and fall in love with. Earlier in the day, he had an opportunity to park his car on Seventh Avenue, and just sit and take in his environment. It was early Sunday morning, and there were black families headed to church, wearing their Sunday's best. John loved seeing so many of his people together, and striving to do well. He never had that opportunity in the south.

As he daydreamed about the past, his thoughts drifted to Doc, and the fact that he hadn't heard from him since he left a few days ago. He was concerned, because that was out of character for Doc. Since they were reunited, Doc had become his most trusted lieutenant next to Sam. This was due partially to Doc's fearlessness, but also his ability to get others to rationalize and see his point of view by any means. Most of the time, this was done simply by using his gift of gab. But, Doc never hesitated to let the bullets fly if further convincing was needed. John respected that about him. He was fierce, but not an uncontrollable hot head like his younger brother Sam had become.

Back in his apartment, John placed five thick knots of twenties on top of the fifty thousand dollars he had in a shoebox hidden under his bed. He was bringing in close to twenty g's a week alone, just from the various number spots that he collected from weekly. He bankrolled a few others, which also put him close to thirty thousand more in cash flow weekly. To him the game was best played maximizing the inflow of cash while minimizing the work involved.

One thing John noticed was that the more money cats made, the more distanced they became from the struggle that actually helped them obtain their success. John still felt the dry stale taste that exists in your throat when you have no idea where your next meal is going to come from. Even with the money he was seeing, he still cherished each dollar he earned as if it was going to be his last. While in deep thought, he sat on the edge of his bed, and rifled through the knots of money in his shoebox. Other than a modest collection of suits and shoes, he hadn't spent much of his cash on anything else.

As he looked at the money in his shoebox, he knew that he had to find a way to make more. He put on a good front, and knew that the hustlers on the street thought he was bringing in major cash, but he didn't have his crew at that point yet. They was just nigga rich, and John wanted more for them.

Woody had the Italians support, which resulted in access to the cash flow needed to back large bets. Like most of the other hustlers uptown, John couldn't afford to bankroll most large bets. If two or three lucky gamblers hit a straight number back to back, he'd be out of business in a heartbeat. So, he hedged the bets, deciding that the risk was worth the reward of increasing his bank. Scared money didn't make none. He decided that he had to be in it to win it.

John remained in deep thought, thinking about his money, Herbert and his ongoing feud with Suede. Herbert was one of those hustlers who allowed himself to become distanced from the struggle, John thought to himself. And now he was being tested by a real street nigga, and was going to rely on the backwards country nigga to do his dirt.

He laughed out loud at the notion. He was at his best when people underestimated him. He couldn't wait to prove Herbert wrong. But, the only problem was that he couldn't find Suede. He was just as unassuming and reclusive as John was. He barely came out. The only difference was that when he came out, he liked to cause a big spectacle. Drenched in fine ass women and enough jewels to make Liberace jealous, he stole the spotlight every time he decided to hit the town.

Besides the women, he always rolled with more than enough killers to take out a small army. Confronting him wouldn't be easy. John laid back on his bed's firm mattress, still fiddling a knot of money in his hand. Before long, he dozed off thinking about what his next move was going to be.

Less than a half an hour later, a loud rattle on the apartment's door startled John, awakening him out of his light sleep. He hopped out of the bed, and grabbed his piece from off of the night table as he walked towards the door slowly.

Leaning his shoulder up against the wall, he yelled "Who is it?"

There was a brief pause, and then a voice on the other side of the door responded, "It's me, Curt."

John looked out the small peephole, before he unlocked the dead bolt and the latch door lock. After securely placing his pistol in the back of his pants, he slowly opened the door. Curt was standing in the hallway with an older black man that appeared to be about twice his age.

"Curt, who's this?" John asked angrily. The older gentleman was about to answer, when John cut him off and said, "No disrespect, but I wasn't talking to you."

"John, this man here be Mr. Hedge Reed," Curt said.

"And? Didn't I tell you not to ever bring anyone around here? Damn! You gotta be the dumbest nigga I know. Where's my brother?"

John's angry words left Curt visibly shaken. He paused before responding, trying to choose his response carefully in order to avoid more of John's wrath.

"Actly, Sam be da one done told me to bring Mr. Hedge Reed over chair."

John glanced over at the old man who was quietly standing in the hallway, scratching his scalp through his thick gray hair. Mr. Reed kept his head down, in order to avoid eye contact with John.

"How do you know he ain't the man Curt?" John asked.

"Oh, I can assure you that I'm not a police officer," Hedge Reed responded politely.

John looked him up and down, and then motioned him into the apartment. As Mr. Reed walked in, John coldly said, "I promise you that if you are a pig, you won't leave this apartment alive."

After John securely locked the door, he sat in a recliner in the living room, joining Curt and Mr. Reed who were already sitting on the leather couch. John pulled his pistol out of the back of his pants, and placed it on the coffee table, spinning it around until it pointed directly towards Mr. Reed.

"What can I help you with?" John asked, while looking Mr. Reed in the eyes.

"I heard a lot about you. You're the man responsible for getting rid of that scum Woody Davis, right?"

John leaned forward in his recliner and said, "I don't know what you're talking about Mr. I'm just a businessman trying to make an honest day's pay."

Mr. Reed cracked a smile. He had heard all about John and how his killers did away with Woody, but he wasn't going to press the issue. "Me too. That's the reason why I'm here. I'm looking to do a little business with you."

"So, what can I do for you?"

"I'm looking to borrow a little money."

John's eyes lit up as he responded, "Oh really? What's a little?"

"About ten thousand dollars worth," Mr. Reed responded. Curt glanced over to see if John's facial expression changed, but he looked unmoved. John was about to respond when Mr. Reed interjected.

"I'm good for it. I'm going to use the money to start my own numbers spot and—"

John stuck his hand out, stopping him mid-sentence. "No need to explain. I know you're good for it. If you've heard enough about me to ask for the money, you already know that if I don't get it back, you're as good as dead," John said in a harsh tone, pausing as he stood up and pulled a knot of hundreds out of his pocket. "Ten thousand today equals twenty thousand in a month."

"Twenty?" Mr. Reed asked in astonishment, his facial expression reflecting disbelief.

"Take it or leave it, old man. It really don't make a damn difference to me," John said coldly.

"I'll take it. But, can I at least get an extra week to pay it back?"

John tossed two rubber band wrapped knots of fifties over to Mr. Reed and said, "I'll see you in a month."

Mr. Reed stood up and graciously shook his hand. As he turned to walk towards the door, he said, "Thank you, very much. I...I don't want to come across as being unappreciative, but I just have one more thing to ask."

"What's that?"

"Well I have two cousins on their way up from Detroit, looking to get into the numbers game as well. I was wondering if you could front them a loan as well?"

"So, you starting your own little family business? Ain't nothing wrong with that. I'll tell you what. Have them see me or my brother Sam once they get into town. I'll take care of them."

"Thanks John, I won't forget this," Mr. Reed responded appreciatively.

John nodded his head, as Mr. Reed grabbed his hand and shook it vigorously again. John smiled and said, "New York ain't an easy town to start up a business in. They can't spect to just come in and set up shop without some manpower. They definitely need to come see me once they get in town. I'll make sure they don't get too much trouble from the local thugs."

The old man nodded and said, "I'll have them see you as soon as they arrive."

As Curt walked out the door behind Mr. Reed, John patted him on the back to let him know that he had done well. Curt cracked a slight grin, and let out a sigh of relief as he made his way out of the building with Mr. Reed.

Protection money was chump change, but John didn't mind providing bodies to keep local thugs at bay. Besides, he knew that if any of the cats he provided protection to found themselves in a bind, he'd be happy to step in and take their businesses off of their hands.

John locked his door and headed back into his bedroom. He smiled as he thought about the money making prospects that the future now held. His little brother had come through. An hour ago, he was trying to think up a scam to bring in some more money, and now he was bankrolling loans charging one hundred percent interest. He knew if he could continue to broker loans, he could turn it into a lucrative business.

As he sat on his bed, he put those thoughts aside, his mind drifting back to Suede. He still hadn't figured out how to track him down and get Herbert's money. And his time was running short.

♦

Sam double parked his egg shell white Cadillac Eldorado in front *The Red Room* on 123 and 7th. *The Red Room* was a jazz club that was frequented by whites and the Negro elite. It was one of those places where you would find hustlers, pimps, athletes and singers all socializing together on any given night. It didn't matter what your profession was here. All that mattered was that you had the cash for the cover charge, and were able to afford the hefty cost for the top shelf liquor that stocked the three luxurious bars positioned throughout the ritzy establishment.

There was a small line outside, but Sam bypassed those waiting anxiously in the cold, and made his way to the front entrance. The bouncer Eddie immediately acknowledged him, slapping him five on his right hand that sported a large diamond studded pinky ring.

"Damn, that's some fly ass ring, my man!" Eddie shouted out.

Sam smiled and downplayed it, responding, "Ah, it ain't nothing." He knew he was looking fly as hell, and he loved the attention. He had bought some new threads from *Ory's* on 125th earlier that day, and he looked like he was skating across the floor in his fly new gators.

The inside of the spacious club was packed. Sam heard someone say that Wilt had stopped in before heading to his big game at the Garden, and there were definitely plenty of fine freaks in the house. He wasn't there for the freaks though. He slowly made his way to the bar, and ordered the finest aged bourbon. The dim lights created a nice mood and ambience that was undeniable. After the bartender fixed his drink, he left a twenty-dollar tip and headed towards the rear of the club, choosing to walk between the tables in order to avoid the crowd on the dance floor.

Tall and handsome, the women stared seductively at Sam, vying to get his attention. But, he just strutted smoothly between those gathered about, not veering off course from his destination. After a dozen or so strides, he reached the door to a secluded room at the rear of the club. He took a long sip from his drink, and firmly pressed the bell located on the wall next to the door. After a minute or so passed, a metal eye level slot in the door slid open and a man looked out. Recognizing Sam, he quickly opened the door and politely escorted him in.

This was where the real action went down, and the real reason why the club was called the *Red Room*. There was a five hundred dollar cover charge just to enter this room, and only the real high rollers and gamblers even knew it existed. Sam slid a knot to the doorman and walked into the small room, as the thick reinforced steel door slammed with a loud thud behind him. There was another bar in here, specifically for the gamblers.

Scantily clad freaks were gathered about, sitting on some of the hustlers' laps and draped over the shoulders of others. The drinks cost twice as much back here, as they did inside the regular club. Sam finished off the drink he brought in with him and immediately ordered another bourbon. The liquor was starting to rush to his head now, and he was enjoying the affects of the high.

Four round wooden tables adorned the mid-sized room, providing comfortable seating for the twenty or more gamblers that were situated about. Sam scanned the room as he lit his cigarette and took a few pulls from it, thinking about where he wanted to make some green.

There was already a smoky haze that filled the air, which was a cloudy mixture of thick cigarette and marijuana smoke that could visibly be seen floating under the dim recessed lights in the ceiling. He looked past the poker tables, not wanting to try his luck at a game he just learned to play a month ago. He didn't feel that his skills were on par with the other high rollers in the room just yet.

Squinting his eyes, he finally focused in on a blackjack table located on the far end of the room. He took another pull from his cigarette, before he made his way past the poker tables and took an empty seat next to a young hustler in the middle of a blackjack hand.

"Sam Skeet, good to see you again baby," the attractive female dealer named Mia said, smiling politely.

Sam just nodded his head in acknowledgment and pulled five thousand dollars worth of bills out of his pant's pocket. The dealer waited until the hand was finished being played, and exchanged his money for a hand full of chips. The minimum blackjack bet was one thousand a hand. Sam was now holding on to five purple chips, which he placed down on the table in front of him.

"Are you in this round?" The dealer asked Sam.

"Yeah, baby," Sam responded confidently. He studied Mia's pretty hands as she dealt him two cards, and swiftly slid two to the young hustler sitting next to him. Sam looked down at his hand and shook his head in disgust.

"Damn, if you wanted to screw me baby, all you had to do was say it," Sam said sarcastically as he laid his cards down.

The young guy next to him laughed out loud, as Mia sucked her teeth and frowned up her face.

"Do you want another card, or what?" She asked Sam.

"Yeah, you might as well hit me. These cards is useless," Sam responded.

Mia reached down and grabbed a card out of the deck in front of her and passed it to Sam. When he turned it over and saw that it was a five of spades, he cracked a smile.

Sam leaned towards the guy sitting next to him and said, "How you looking my man?"

The young hustler looked down at his hand and asked for another card. She hit him with an eight of diamonds. He threw his cards down, revealing a king of spades and a four of spades. Mia had a jack of clubs exposed already. She turned over her second card that was lying face down, revealing a ten of hearts. A smile came over her face. She looked over to Sam, who was puffing from his cancer stick slowly. He turned over his cards revealing a ten of clubs and a six of diamonds, to go along with the five Mia just dealt him.

"That looks like blackjack sweetie," he said in a cocky fashion.

"You are one lucky sonofabitch," Mia responded, as she collected the cards and passed him ten purple chips.

Sam took five of the chips off of the table and blew a kiss at Mia before he said, "Hmmm, and I thought you were trying to screw me."

"Maybe I am," she responded as she licked her thick lips and begin dealing a new hand. Midway through dealing, Mel the manager of the gambling area of the *Red Room* strolled over. He had been watching everything that had been going on from across the room, and didn't like the body language he saw Sam and Mia exhibiting.

"I'll finish dealing this hand," Mel said to Mia.

Sam smiled and took a sip from his bourbon. "Damn, I didn't expect to see you so soon Mel. I only won ten thousand from you so far," he said confidently.

"Well, let's just see how lucky you are now," Mel responded, as he turned over one of the cards he dealt to himself, revealing an ace of hearts.

Sam looked down at his cards, quickly thinking whether or not he wanted to take another card. He slowly scanned the room through his unfocused eyes. The room had gotten packed since he started playing blackjack. The sea of bodies only came across as blurry objects, until Sam's eyes locked with another very familiar pair. It was Black, Suede's right hand man that he had a run in with a few weeks back. He had two other men with him that were trying to blend in with the small crowd.

Black glared at Sam, his left eye twitching uncontrollably out of nervousness mixed with anger. They stared at each other for a split second, before Sam put his cards down in front of him revealing his hand. He had a ten of diamonds and a nine of hearts.

Mel had turned over his second card, revealing a seven of clubs. He needed at least a two to beat Sam's hand. He went to the deck and came up with a four of diamonds. Sam laughed out loud when he saw the card Mel pulled. Mel's facial expression was full of disgust. He turned red with anger.

"Damn Mel, I ain't never seen you turn so red," Sam said as he cracked a huge grin. "You look like a big Italian lobster."

Everyone in an earshot laughed out loud. As Sam collected his chips, Black quietly slid in behind him. Sam was oblivious to his movements, and was caught off guard when he turned around and was greeted by Black's tall frame hovering in front of him. He slipped his hand down into his pocket unnoticed, and gripped his piece. He was prepared for whatever.

"What's up Sam? Long time no see nigga," Black said as he stared directly into Sam's face.

"I'm doing good man," Sam said smiling, as he paused to sip from his drink. "You must be good luck Black. I mean, every time I see you I'm winning shit."

Black frowned up his face as anger began to build up inside of him. Sam had a smug grin on his face that was only adding more fuel to the fire.

"You know you didn't win that dice game, right nigga?" Black asked coldly.

Sam laughed to himself. He noticed Black getting upset, and thought that it was funny as hell.

"You're probably right Black," Sam said, pausing to sip from his glass slowly. "But, who really gives a fuck. Last I checked, there was only one team with a score on the scoreboard…and it wasn't yours nigga."

Just as Sam finished his sentence, one of Black's boys walked over from the poker table and whispered something in his air. After they went back and forth whispering for a few seconds, Black angrily looked back over to Sam.

"We'll finish this shit later," Black muttered, as he turned and began to walk towards the poker table near the back of the room.

"Yeah, I'm a get back to gambling your money," Sam said, humoring himself further.

He gambled for an hour or so more, downing a bottle of bourbon and giving back most of his winnings before he left the Red Room's gambling area. The music was still going strong, and the dance floor was even more packed as Sam stumbled drunkenly back into the main area of the club. He looked around the room and started walking towards the bar. He wanted one more drink before he headed back to his apartment.

As he walked between a couple of tables, someone tapped him lightly on the shoulder. "Excuse me," could faintly be heard over the loud music. Sam turned around slowly, and was greeted by a beautiful light skinned female wearing a skintight dress. She was obviously five or six years older than him and built like a stallion. He looked her up and down, admiring her toned legs and wide hips. She stood confidently in front of him as he lusted over her.

"I was just about to get me another drink. What are you sipping on?" Sam asked.

"Oh, this is a martini," she said, as she sipped the last drop of her drink through a thin straw before finishing her sentence. "But, I don't want another drink though. I wanna go somewhere and fuck."

She licked her lips seductively as the words left her mouth, catching Sam visibly off guard as his drink went down the wrong pipe. He rebounded quickly, and countered her advance by saying, "I can dig it...then let's get the fuck outta here."

She smiled and grabbed his hand, leading him towards the front of the club. He followed behind her, focusing on her thick ass as it jiggled under her dress with each step she took. The dress accentuated every curve on her hourglass shaped body, and he glorified in the fact that he was walking with the finest female in the club.

En route to the door, a fine looking brown skinned female approached and whispered something in the ear of the female walking with Sam. She was also incredibly beautiful, with flawless unblemished chocolate skin. Sam undressed her perfect body with his eyes. The girls went back and forth for a few minutes conversing, before they looked over to Sam.

"Do you mind dropping my friend Zora off? We have to pass her house on the way to my apartment," the female said, still holding Sam's hand tightly.

"Yeah, I can do that," he said, while staring into her deep brown eyes. "I know her name, and I don't even know yours."

"It's Marie baby."

"Don't you want to know mine?" Sam asked curiously.

"Nah, just get me home. Tonight, I'm a just call you Daddy."

Sam's dick got hard as she led him to the coat check, where the two women retrieved their jackets. Then they walked outside the club, where there was still a short line of people waiting to get in. Shivering from the night air, the girls followed closely behind Sam. He walked to his car and unlocked the front and back passenger's doors for the two females, before heading around to the driver's side of the car.

Eddie the bouncer was nosily looking on, observing the whole scene.

"Damn, you had to grab up two Skeet? Greedy motherfucker." he said sarcastically.

Sam just nodded his head and cracked a smile before saying, "Be cool baby."

He started the car and pulled off down the street. Marie had told him that her friend lived by Riverside Park, so he headed in that direction. He looked in his rear view mirror and caught Zora's eyes staring intently back at him. She winked at him and licked her lips, when she noticed that she had caught his attention. Sam smiled back. His senses were numb, and he was still feeling the affects of the liquor.

Marie put her right foot on his dashboard as he drove. She grabbed his freehand and placed it on her left leg, guiding it up her smooth thigh, until he reached her wet vagina. He played with her clitoris slowly as she moaned. She wasn't wearing any underwear beneath her tight dress.

"I can't wait, Daddy," she whispered in a seductive moan. Sam was fingering her gently now, and she was gyrating her waist driving his fingers deeper inside of her.

"Pull over here and fuck me Daddy," Marie whispered. Sam was enjoying every minute of it. He continued fingering her, as he felt a light kiss on the back of his neck. He glanced in the rear view mirror again, and saw Zora sitting right behind him. Her blouse was pulled up, exposing her large and very firm breasts.

"After you fuck her, I want you to fuck me," Zora whispered softly into his ear. Sam felt like he was about to bust on himself. He drove around until he found a dark and quiet block, parked and turned off the car.

Marie immediately unzipped his pants and begin massaging his manhood in her soft hands, until it hardened in her palms. Zora was sucking lightly on the back of his neck, making him even more aroused. Resting his back in the seat, he closed his eyes and started daydreaming about anything that would keep him from coming. This was like a fantasy. He had never been with two women before, and the thought alone had him on edge.

"Can I kiss it for you?" Marie asked, as she gripped his penis tightly in her hand. Her thick wet lips were inches away from his manhood. Sam gasped, before replying, "Yeah."

As he pushed her head down into his lap, he looked in the rear view mirror at Zora. Now she was leaning back in her seat, fidgeting between her legs. Sam figured she was getting off on herself, as she waited for him to finish with Marie. He couldn't wait to get inside of that freak.

Marie took him deep inside her throat, as he moaned from the feeling of her wet saliva and the pressure she was applying on him with her tongue and mouth. She was bobbing up and down quickly, taking him in deeper and deeper. Sam was oblivious to everything going on around him. The liquor and Marie's sexual escapades had him in a state of pure bliss. As he struggled to maintain his composure, he thought about the freak sitting in the backseat again. He couldn't come yet. He wanted to wait until he had Zora.

Glancing in the rearview mirror again, his blurry eyes noticed a sudden movement in the darkness. His instincts kicked into action quickly, causing him to forcefully push Marie to the side and reach into his pocket for his piece. As he fiddled around for his gun, Zora delivered a vicious blow from a billy club to the side of his head. A pain like he had never felt before exploded throughout his body. His arms and legs went limp, as Zora delivered a second blow to his crown.

Marie quickly searched his pockets until she came up with his money clip. Sam slipped into an unconscious state as the shrieking tires of a car pulling up next to him could be heard loudly echoing on the quiet street. A male yelled, "Hurry up," as the girls quickly exited and jumped into the awaiting car. Seconds later, the tires shrieked again as the car quickly pulled off down the street, vanishing into the darkness of the night.

In his mid-sized apartment, John sat at the makeshift woodworker's desk that he had assembled in the spare bedroom. When he had the time, he would sit down behind the desk and carve a sculpture out of soft wood. This was a skill that his father passed down to him, and a talent that he had become very proficient at over the years. Growing up poor, he didn't have access to the set of tools that a typical craftsman would use. But, he made due with his sharpened knife, skillfully sculpting busts and other beautiful works of art.

Admiring his craftsmanship, he carefully examined the carved wooden sculpture of an African princess that he held in his hand. He thought about his brother Sam, concerned that he hadn't heard from him since earlier in the day. He was pissed off that Curt had let Sam go off on his own. His exploits around Harlem had earned him a name for himself.

Hustlers knew about Sam Skeet, and John knew that his notoriety could easily result in his demise.

After pacing back and forth in deep thought, John called Curt at his pad and sent him out looking for Sam. John was infuriated, but kept his composure as he loaded his piece and prepared to hit the streets. It was times like this that he missed Doc. Doc would've stayed on top of Sam, keeping his crazy ass out of trouble.

John tucked his .45 in the back of his pants, threw on his leather trench coat and unlocked the front door to his apartment. His attention was immediately diverted down the hallway, as he heard a loud noise. In the shadows, he saw Sam staggering down the hallway, bumping up against the wall as he struggled to make it to the apartment. His heart dropped to the bowels of his stomach, as he looked at his brother stumbling towards him. As John frantically ran over to Sam, he thought about his father's savage murder.

Deep red blood drenched Sam's linen shirt, and continued to pour out of the large gash on the side of his forehead. John grabbed him in his arms tightly, just as his eyes rolled back and he collapsed from the loss of blood.

CHAPTER 9

Sam only had to spend a few hours at Harlem hospital, where the medics stitched him up and monitored him closely until they were satisfied that he hadn't suffered a concussion. He was put on an iron supplement, to help build up the significant amount of blood that he had lost. More than anything, his pride had been deeply bruised. He couldn't wait to get back out on the streets, so he could murder the foul bitches that had set him up. But, after three weeks passed, he accepted the fact that they had probably skipped town with his bread. The thought alone made him even more infuriated.

John however, couldn't give a damn about the money that was stolen. After Sam recovered from his near brush with death, he became very protective of his younger brother, keeping him by his side as much as possible. A two-inch scar was tattooed to the side of Sam's temple, which served as a constant reminder of the vicious blows he was dealt by the billy club.

John got a kick out of riding him whenever he got the chance, joking that he was the only nigga he knew that had to get stitches from a little bitch slap. He struggled to make as much light of the incident as he could, but he was definitely concerned. It was three weeks ago, but he was still haunted by the fact that he could have lost his baby brother.

They weren't the same broke ass country boys who traveled to New York with big dreams over a year ago. They had made a name for themselves now. They were also seeing some bread as well, and there were carnivorous vultures on the prowl just waiting to swoop down and take their shit if they let them.

Even though bright yellow sunrays shot through the clouds, it was deceivingly cold outside. The heat blasted out of the vents in the car, as John drove around making his usual money collections, with Sam riding shotgun and Stink Harris sitting in the back. Stink was a childhood friend of Sam's that had come up from the south a couple of months earlier, and quickly earned John's respect due to the way he handled himself on the streets. There were over a dozen cats that John brought up from the south, but only a few like Stink were considered part of the inner circle. Normally Doc would have been with him, but John still hadn't heard from him.

Lately, the money from bankrolling loans had begun to pick up drastically. It was amazing how many people needed money for gambling debts, numbers, business ventures and other types of miscellaneous reasons. As they drove down the streets of Harlem, Sam peered out the window, taking in the sights. Beautiful women were always in abundance on the Harlem streets, and their attention was always seized by a nigga with a hot set of wheels.

As Sam continued to look around, he noticed Lucky, a local gambler that had borrowed a thousand dollars from John a couple of weeks earlier. He was strolling down the street hand in hand with a pretty black female. Sam excitedly tapped John on his shoulder as he said, "There's that motherfucker Lucky right there. He's been ducking us for weeks."

As John pulled up to a red light and waited for it to turn green, Lucky and his girlfriend walked right past the front of his car as they crossed the street. Lucky's frightened eyes met John's, once he noticed the shiny Cadillac beside him. Sam grabbed the door handle, ready to jump out of the car and whoop his ass, but John held him back by grabbing his left arm forcefully.

"Relax baby…just relax," John said calmly. Noticeably agitated, Sam pulled away.

"We should get that motherfucker now, John!" Sam yelled angrily.

"Nah, let that motherfucker be. We'll see him again."

"If we just let that nigga be, everybody gonna think they can just dip out on us with our cash."

John sighed, before saying, "Sam, a dead man can't pay back his debts."

"Yeah, but a crippled nigga can pay back his green just fine."

Stink and John chuckled out loud, before John said, "That man is out with his girl. We'll see his ass again. It ain't like he moving outta Harlem or something. There's some things you just don't do."

Unconvinced, Sam shrugged his shoulders and mumbled something incoherently under his breath. John ignored him, and pulled off down the street once the light changed. Even though Lucky was ducking him, he didn't believe in disrespecting a man in front of his family in order to collect on a debt. Business was business, and John felt that there were rules to the game that needed to be followed. He never wavered from this belief.

They stopped at *Jive Talk*, which was the new name for Woody's old bar, renamed in honor of the man that now ran it. This was one of the few number's spots that John actually played a hands on role in the day to day operations. He preferred to stay behind the scenes, never wanting to bring too much attention to himself. But, he enjoyed visiting Jive Talk and chatting it up with him for hours on end. They had immediately hit it off on that fateful day when he had his first and last conversation with Woody.

Jive reminded him of his deceased father, and being that he had spent so much of his life in the presence of hustlers, John liked to lean on him to increase his own knowledge of the game. Jive loved the attention. It was the first time in a while that someone actually valued his opinion. The local hustlers had never shown him respect in the past. So, he willingly became a mentor to John. Marveling at how he soaked up everything he shared with him like a sponge.

Jive was a new man nowadays. The old man that complained constantly about the shrapnel in his knees, was rejuvenated by his newfound responsibilities. He strutted around the bar in expensive suits, spitting his old time game to the young hoes who loved to flock around him in hordes. Jive gave them drinks on the house, or even slid them some green every now and then. Whatever it took to get them up to his office and get a quick feel. Jive was living his second childhood, but he never let his extracurricular activities get in the way of business. John respected that about him.

After chatting it up with Jive for a while, John, Stink and Sam headed over to *Rubie's Diner* to have an early afternoon lunch with Bilal. Bilal's Black Muslim movement was steadily making strides in Harlem, as young males and females rallied behind his group in search of a cause. Trading in their latest digs for concealing veils that covered their heads or clean suits, the youth had completely accepted the Muslim's strict principles and ideals.

John marveled at how Bilal had completely adopted the ideals and got so many to follow him. They sat at the same table that was always reserved for Bilal in the back of the diner, sipping on some homemade iced tea. John took a bite out of a piece of buttery cornbread that was in a basket in the middle of the table.

"You remember Miss. Lucy that was always preaching that Jesus was on his way?" John asked Bilal.

Bilal laughed before saying, "Yeah, everyone thought she was crazy and would try to avoid having to speak to her, right?"

"Yeah, well that's my man Stink's mom," John responded with a sarcastic grin on his face.

"I apologize, I didn't mean anything by —" Bilal said embarrassingly, before being interrupted mid-sentence by Stink.

"There's no need to be apologizing. My mama is crazy as hell," Stink said, as everyone at the table broke out in laughter.

After the laughter simmered down, John looked over to Bilal and asked, "So, how's the bean pie business treating you?"

"The word is being spread as quickly as possible, you know? I mean, spiritual enlightenment doesn't happen overnight. It can take a lifetime to turn a sinner into a righteous man, but only a second for a righteous man to sin," Bilal responded.

"And how's the money?" Sam asked inquisitively. He had been admiring the sharp suit Bilal was wearing ever since they first walked into the restaurant.

"Money? Well, Allah provides. When I lay my burdens on him, he quickly responds," Bilal responded confidently.

"Must be good," John said.

"Yes it is. I just prayed to him this morning and asked that he provide an outlet for our restless youth. I know he'll respond shortly," Bilal said.

"What kind of outlet?" John asked.

"A youth center or something of that sort. There's so many dangerous paths that our youth can encounter when they don't have a constructive means to channel their energy."

"Listen, I'd like to be a part of something like that," John said excitedly as his eyes lit up.

Bilal's face frowned up noticeably. He took a huge gulp from his iced tea and said, "John don't take this the wrong way, but you know I can't mix Allah's goals with Satan's will."

John was taken aback by his friend's cold response, but he didn't show it. His demeanor remained the same as he responded, "Bilal, if you are truly doing the work of God, you would want to help positive things come out of those things that you deem to be evil. Now, if I'm a sinner making sinful money, that I only share with fellow sinners...Satan wins. Right?"

"And, what are you getting at Johnny?"

"The mentally and spiritually blind, as you call them, are always going to give their money to people like me. I just want a chance to turn something negative into something positive. Allah would approve of that, right? "

"Now, you bringing Allah into it. Now you're Muslim, huh? Spit it out Johnny. What are you saying?" Bilal asked impatiently.

"I have ten thousand that's just sitting around collecting dust. Use it for your youth center," John said.

"Johnny, I can't do that. I…I just wouldn't feel comfortable with being partners with a numbers runner," Bilal said.

"Listen, I don't want to be partners with you, as much as you don't want to be partners with me. I just want to put my money towards something positive. Let me help you out, Bilal," John said pleadingly.

"What about the pigs John. If they find out I'm getting backed by you, they—"

"You don't have to worry about that. I give you my word. I'm simply providing funding. Other than that, you don't have nothing to be concerned with," John said confidently.

Bilal sat in deep concentration for a few seconds that seemed like an eternity, before holding his hand out to John. "You've got a deal Johnny. I've trusted you up until now, and I always will."

John enthusiastically grabbed his hand and shook it aggressively as he said, "Here you go!"

He thrust a folded white envelope into Bilal's hand. The envelope had ten thousand dollars in it, and already had Bilal's name written on it.

"Johnny, you sly dog. You came over here intending to give me money. How'd you know I would accept your offer?" Bilal asked.

"I didn't. But, I wanted to be prepared just in case," John responded.

This was the first time he gave Bilal money, but it wouldn't be the last. Bilal called one of his bodyguards over, and handed him the envelope while he gave him some quick instructions. The bodyguard placed the envelope in his suit pocket, walking off just as Bilal and John embraced, celebrating their agreement.

After completing their daily runs, John and Sam dropped Stink off and returned back to their apartment. They planned on sitting around the pad for the rest of the day, and finishing up a game of chess they started playing the night before. John was known for his chess playing prowess, and even though Sam was skillful as well, he had never won a game against him. Nonetheless, he bet John five hundred dollars that he would win. They both sat at the glass table in the dining room focused, staring at the beautifully crafted wooden chess pieces John had carved. It was Sam's turn, and he was carefully analyzing the board, trying to anticipate how John would react to his next move. He rubbed the scar on his forehead, as he thought out his move.

"*KnockKnockKnockKnock*", a rattling at the door broke Sam's concentration. He jumped up from the table and looked out the peephole. It was Curt, who was standing in the hallway with a huge dumb looking smile on his face. Sam quickly opened the door and motioned for Curt to come in, but he just stood there, still smiling from ear to ear.

Sam started to walk back to the table, but stopped and turned around when he realized Curt wasn't following behind him. "Curt, what the hell is wrong witchu nigga? Get your ole' simple ass in here boy."

"I gots me a surprise," Curt said, still cracking a wide smile.

"Good, bring the shit inside and close the door nigga."

"I can't. This dear surprise bees too big."

Visibly losing his patience, Sam yelled, "Listen nigga, just bring—"

His sentence was interrupted as a man with a very familiar face walked in front of Curt and said, "You ain't changed a bit. Never did have a lick of patience."

Sam's face nearly dropped to the floor as his oldest brother Willie walked towards him. His face had thinned out since Sam last saw him, but he looked the same as he remembered, as he limped into the apartment noticeably favoring his left leg. Hearing the commotion, John walked into the living room as well.

"Damn, both my baby brother's looking good as hell. What it be like baby?" Willie asked.

John's eyes welled up with tears. He hadn't seen his older brother in ages. As the situation worsened in the South, and they struggled to survive through constant bouts with poverty, Willie enlisted into the Army. John was forced to provide for his family, as his mother slowly deteriorated and succumbed to her eventual death. His emotions were mixed, as anger began to build up inside of him.

The anger quickly subsided as he looked at his brother closely. Willie's suit was dirty and noticeably tattered. His cheekbones were visibly pronounced, through the skin of his drawn in face. John's thoughts drifted back to the bouts with starvation he had experienced less than two years ago. As much as he hated the fact that Willie left him and Sam to fend for themselves, he still loved him. Seeing his brother like this made him sad.

"Stop lookin' at me like that John," Willie said as he limped over to him and gave him a hug. "Shit, those slanty-eyed gooks tried to shoot off my motherfuckin' leg, but they missed the one that the bitches care about. Ya, dig? And when I'm tearing up some pussy, that's the only motherfuckin' leg that matters."

Everyone in the room broke out into a loud laughter. Willie's time away had obviously changed him. He had spent a lot of time with enlisted men from all around the country, and he had adopted their terminologies and mannerisms. He didn't act or sound like the southern boy who joined the army years ago. He was always cocky, but now he had a certain cocky swagger about him.

"Man, those motherfuckin' peckerwood cops had it in for Doc man," Willie said.

John's facial expression became confused. He hadn't heard from Doc since he went down south, and was surprised to hear Willie mention his name.

"What?" John asked perplexed. Confused with the sudden change of topic.

"Yeah, I knew shit was gonna hit the fan when he rolled into town in that fancy ride he had. When we had spoke a few weeks back, I told him I would take a bus up here and shit. But, motherfuckin' Doc was insistent on picking us up," Willie said.

"You spoke to Doc a few weeks ago?" John asked in an astonished tone.

"Yeah, I got your number from crazy old Ms. Lucy."

"Where's he at now?" John asked, his voice sounding very concerned.

"Like I said, motherfuckin' peckerwoods was after that nigga. They gave him a year for some outstanding warrant they said he had. If you ask me, it was some bullshit. They was just jealous of that nigga coming back to town, showing off wit a new car and shit."

John's face dropped, as he mumbled, "Damn." His feeling of excitement was dulled as he heard the news of his friend's fate. He had wondered why Doc was so insistent about heading down south by himself, and why he had been so secretive. Now it turned out that he got locked up because he was trying to surprise him. This upset John deeply. He knew how racist the cops in the south were. A sentence for a year could easily result in life, if those red-necked crackers really had it in for you. His mind drifted off, already thinking of a way to get his friend out of jail.

Curt was still standing out in the hallway with the same dumb looking smile on his face he had since he first knocked on the door. He leaned his hefty body against the doorframe, as he stood by silently. Sam's attention shifted from his brothers, as he glanced over to the doorway, noticing Curt still standing there. He told him to come inside, but Curt still stayed leaning against the doorframe, not moving an inch.

Finally, Curt stood straight up and said, "Dat dear ain't da only saprize."

His voice sounded real childish and giddy like. Everyone in the room focused their attention on him, as he walked into the room slowly, purposely leaving the door open. A pretty young female holding a toddler in her arms walked in behind him. It was Michelle, John's girlfriend that he left behind when he came to Harlem. He hadn't spoken to her in two years, but her smooth brown skin was just as beautiful as he remembered.

He thought back to the first day he laid eyes on her walking down a dirt road in Williston. Not only beautiful, she also impressed John with her sincere innocence. Nothing had ever been given to John. Nothing in his life was ever pure, except his mother...and Michelle. She still had that look of innocence in her deep brown eyes that melted his heart when he stared into them.

Walking towards her, he looked at the eyes of the young boy that she held in her arms. No older than a year and a half or so, he had something very familiar about him. As John crept closer, a tear slowly ran down Michelle's brown cheek.

"He's yours, John. His name is Andre. Andre Williams. I gave him my daddy's first name," Michelle said, just as her emotions gave way and she let out an uncontrollable cry. John rushed to her, kissing her on her wet cheek as he wrapped his arm around her and his son. Everyone looked on, as he held them both tightly, tears coming down his face as well.

"Why didn't you tell me? Why didn't you let me know you were pregnant?" John asked.

"I found out a month after you left. I knew that things weren't going good. I knew you was trying hard, but I didn't want you to have to worry about a child too."

"You should have told me though babe…you should have let me know," John said, as he kissed her on her forehead lightly. A smile came over his face, as he grabbed his son out of her arms and excitedly said, "Andre Williams. I got me a son yawl! I got me a son!"

The mood of excitement and disbelief continued to fill the night as the old friends celebrated, and reminisced about the past. John spent most of the night alone in his bedroom with Michelle and Andre. Even though he hadn't kept in contact with Michelle, she was always in his heart. He hadn't been with another woman since the last night they spent together, and ironically that was most likely when she conceived.

Michelle couldn't believe how much John had matured in the time since he left. He was always an old soul, but the boy that left her with promises of a better life up north over two years ago, was now unmistakably a man. John held his son firmly in his arms, and stared into his face admiring his good looks. He remembered his own father picking him up and holding him when he was younger.

As a child his father held him in his big strong arms, and he naively thought that his old man was invincible. His father was a sharecropper who worked day in and day out for scraps. But, he did his best with what the white folks would give him. Proud and dignified, he didn't ask for anything more than what any man would expect in life. But, he was a nigger. And when a nigger got out of line, a nigger got murdered. Regretfully, John and Willie witnessed their father's brutal murder. The long lasting effects taking more of a toll on Willie, who battled the demons from the past daily.

John sat quietly as his thoughts became clouded with visions of the tragic events that led to his father's untimely demise. Sensing something was wrong, Michelle sat on the bed next to him and kissed him lightly on the forehead.

She ran her hand across his face and said, "I missed you John. I thought that you didn't love me anymore."

"I thought about you everyday, babe...everyday. You don't ever have to question my love for you," he responded, staring deeply into her eyes.

"Then why didn't I hear from you? Why did you have me sitting down there wondering if you were dead? Not knowing if I was ever going to see you again?" She asked, her bottom lip quivering uncontrollably. She had spent many a night crying herself to sleep, worried about him.

"Stop crying, baby. Stop crying," John said, as he wrapped one of his arms around her. His face became very serious. "I don't wanna see you like this. But, I gotta be truthful with you Michelle. Baby, I wasn't thinking about you everyday. Not because I don't love you, but because I couldn't. It's like Doc, being locked up and shit. The only way you make it through your time is to forget about those on the outside, and focus on the shit going on around you. I'd be dead if I was thinking about you...*about us* everyday."

"But, John—"

"But, nothing Michelle. I was embarrassed as a man. I had big plans for us, and shit just wasn't working out. I couldn't face you."

She leaned in towards him and kissed him on the cheek. "You don't ever have to be embarrassed with me John. You know I don't care about money. I would be broke with you. I would starve with you," her voice cracked, and her southern accent sounded more pronounced. "Promise me you'll never do that to me again."

"I'll never leave you alone again babe," John said as he kissed her on her forehead and looked down at little Andre. "I can't believe this little critter looks just like me!"

"Especially, around the eyes."

"Yeah, he got them cold ass eyes like my pops had!"

Michelle shoved him lightly on his shoulder.

"John Williams, you need to wash your mouth out with soap. You done came up to New York and became all gutter mouthed like a sailor."

John laughed out loud before saying, "Yeah, I know. I need to get my shi—, I mean my stuff straight!"

In the living room, Willie observed Sam, amazed at how grown his little brother had become. He regretted leaving his family alone to fend for themselves, selfishly in search of a way out for himself. As the oldest, growing up Willie had been his father's pride and joy. They had the same facial features and mannerisms, which led most town folk to call Willie "Junior", even though he didn't share his father's name.

Witnessing his father's brutal murder as a child had impacted him greatly. And when his mother was stricken with her illness, he refused to go through the experience of losing someone dear to him again. A huge part of him died back in South Carolina with his father, and he purposely allowed the rest to slowly wither away over the years, as he struggled to come to terms with his death.

The rallying cry in America focused on patriotism and liberation, as young men eagerly enlisted in the army in order to kill the savages abroad. Contrarily, when Willie abandoned his family to join the army, he was in pursuit of a different form of death...assisted suicide. Too fearful to face his own demons, and too cowardly to take his own life, he headed to the battlefields hoping to die.

As he spoke to Sam, he realized how selfish his actions had been. He couldn't get the time he lost with his brothers back. His youngest brother had grown up, without the benefit of two older brothers being around to show him how to become a man.

He was also greatly concerned about Sam's demeanor. His little brother's eyes looked as cold and menacing as the killers he had served duty with on the battlefields of Korea. He shared war stories with Sam and Curt, telling them all about his tour of duty, and the sniper that sent a hot slug ripping through his leg. They listened on intently, very interested in his gruesome war stories.

With the liquor flowing, time passed by quickly. They ended up chatting up a storm into the wee hours of the morning, until they eventually passed out from exhaustion. Sam let Willie take his bed, and he and Curt crashed out on the two sofas in the living room. As the sun rose, the only one still awake was John. Knelling down by the side of his bed, and resting his chin on his two fists, he stared intently at Michelle and Andre as they slept. He still couldn't believe he had a child on this earth. Andre looked just like a spitting image of him. John leaned over and kissed him on his soft pudgy cheek, and promised to never let him suffer through a childhood like he had.

◆

Later that evening, the big city lights illuminated the midtown area of Manhattan as tourists and pedestrians walked about. Petey Wilson stood outside of the *Ambassador Inn*, in his red uniform, waiting patiently for some patrons to stroll in. He had only been in New York for a month before he had the good fortune to land himself a gig at the hotel as a doorman. The pay was decent, and he was making a killing off of the tips he was getting from the rich white folks that frequented the establishment.

When the white folk pulled in front of the hotel, he politely ran up to their cars, making sure he appeared eager to hold the door open for them and carry their bags. They liked seeing a young nigger at their beck and call, and most of them reflected it in their generous tips. He could have never made this type of money in South Carolina, so he felt a great amount of gratitude towards his cousin John, for wiring the money for him to come up north.

Petey knew that his cousin was making money in all types of illegal business, but John never tried to get him involved. This made him feel even more deeply indebted to him. It was like a stroke of pure luck when Petey found himself holding the door open for a young sharply dressed black man that strolled in with two beautiful women that night.

It was a rare occasion to see blacks at *The Ambassador*. They either had to be a sports figure, a movie star or a hustler. Petey probably wouldn't have thought much of this, but one of the sexy black chicks glued to the young man's arm, referred to him as Suede. He was a light skinned pretty boy, about six foot two, with a medium sized build. Dressed in a blue and white pin stripped suit, with a white sky, he was smooth as silk. But, on the streets they simply called him Suede.

Petey heard his cousin make mention of that name before, and felt that it may be worth something to him if he knew Suede was at the hotel. On a few occasions, he had tried to pay John back the money he had wired him, but he always refused. He hoped that he would find this little tidbit of information valuable. It couldn't hurt. Besides, he was eager to return a favor to John.

After escorting Suede and the two fine ass females with him to room 580, and collecting his twenty dollar tip, Petey called John at his apartment. John happened to be home with Michelle and Andre when he called. Petey could hear the excitement in his voice when he shared the news.

It was a little after nine in the evening now, and the customers were starting to roll in. Petey told John that if he waited until after eleven, his boss would be off, and he could sneak him in through the service entrance. John thanked him for the tip, and told him that he would see him at eleven.

Finally, he had gotten his opportunity to approach Suede without his bodyguards being around. He couldn't have been more lucky.

The city that never sleeps had calmed to a considerably slower pace as the evening progressed. By 10:30pm, the cold wintry air had forced most people to seek shelter indoors. Petey finished working the lobby and punched his timecard at 11:00pm, for his fifteen-minute break. Curt and Stink Harris stayed in the car, as John and Sam braved the cold air, waiting patiently in the alleyway for ten minutes or so. They quickly rushed into the service entrance when Petey opened the door, eager to thaw out.

Petey immediately gave John a tight hug when he walked in, and slapped Sam five. Petey was a little older than John. He had gone to grade school with Willie before having to drop out in the fourth grade to find work. They stood in what appeared to be a break room for workers to store their clothes, or get some rest in between shifts. There was a wooden table and some chairs in the middle of the small room, and a metal clothes rack with uniforms, some coats and jackets hanging from it. A service elevator that provided access to every floor in the building was located immediately outside the room in the hallway.

John took his coat off and placed it on a wooden hanger that was on the clothes rack. Sam followed suit, afterwards rubbing his hands together briskly, still feeling the effects of the bitter cold outside.

"Hey Pete, who's uniforms are these?" John asked, as he grabbed the jacket sleeve of one of the uniforms hanging from the clothes rack.

"Nobodies. Just extra just in case we be needing to wear a different one while ours is in the cleaners."

John grabbed a hat and uniform jacket off of the rack and tried it on. The jacket fit him a little big, but it looked fine on him. Sam searched through the remaining uniforms until he found a jacket that fit him as well. He had long irregular arms, so most of the jackets fit him awkwardly. After holding a few up to his chest, he settled for one that fit him tightly and had sleeves that rested slightly above his wrists. Once he squeezed into the jacket, he took his piece out of the back of his pants and placed it in one of the side pockets of the uniform jacket.

"What room is he in?" John asked.

"Room 580, on the fifth floor," Petey responded.

"That service elevator will take me right to that floor?"

"Yeah. The room will be directly down the hall from you."

John began walking towards the elevator door in the hallway, stopping short when he noticed a cart used to transfer lining. There were some neatly folded sheets and pillowcases on top of the cart, and pillows on the bottom shelf. He looked back at Sam, and let out a muffled laugh. The jacket he had on looked like it belonged to a little kid. It has so tight on him that he could barely bend his arms.

"You look like a goddamn idiot," John said sarcastically.

"Fuck you, man!" Sam responded angrily.

John took the pillows off of the bottom of the cart, and threw them in the corner where there was a pile of other bedding. He told Sam to take off the jacket, and to get on the bottom of the cart. Sam gladly peeled the skintight jacket off and climbed carefully onto the bottom of the cart. It was a tight and uncomfortable squeeze, but he was able to fit his long lanky body on the cold metal shelf. John unfolded a sheet and hung it over the sides, effectively hiding Sam.

Petey looked on nervously. He saw Sam pull out his gun earlier, and had no idea what was about to take place. Nonetheless, he felt obligated to ask John, "Do you need my help?"

John smiled at his goodhearted cousin before he replied, "Nah, Petey. You done enough. Go back to work, I don't want you to have no parts in what's about to go down."

Petey reached in his pocket as a thought crossed his mind. "Here John," he said as he remembered the spare key to the suite, that he had lifted earlier from behind the front desk. John excitedly took the key, and thanked his cousin once again.

Petey felt relieved as he held the elevator door open and waited for John to push the cart onto it. When the elevator door closed, Petey let out a quick sigh before he punched his timecard in and headed back to the hotel's entrance. As he stood comfortably at the front door, the butterflies that had been giving his stomach a queasy feeling finally began to subside.

Suede rested his head up against the headboard of the king sized bed, with his eyes slightly closed. One hand was holding a fat Cuban cigar, and the other gripped a handful of the beautiful light skinned girl's hair, helping her bob her head up and down on his dick. The darker complexioned girl lay across the love seat fingering herself and playing with her breasts.

She was a bisexual freak, who loved going down on chicks as much as she liked a penis in her pussy. Her flawless skin complimented her beautiful looks. That was more than enough reason for Suede to keep her on his payroll. Plus it didn't hurt that she had access to plenty of fine females. Even while she lay on the couch getting off on herself, she kept her piece close by in her small handbag.

"Good evening, Maam...and sir," John said as walked past a young white couple, shortly after he got off of the elevator when it reached the fifth floor. He pushed the cart slowly, as he continued down the carpeted hallway following the ascending hotel room numbers. Once he reached 580, he cautiously looked both ways down the hall, before quietly putting the key in the lock and turning the brass doorknob slowly. As he slowly pushed the linen cart into the room, he clutched the gun in his pocket, expecting to be confronted by someone. But, he entered the suite's living room area unheard and unnoticed.

He pushed the metal cart slowly across the marble tile that beautifully adorned the spacious room, trying to make as little noise as possible. Once the cart reached the area rug that was positioned in the middle of the room, he stopped pushing. The wheels were making a creaking sound, and he didn't want to alarm anyone.

A small kitchenette area was off to his right, and the bedroom was located directly in front of him. The door was cracked open slightly. From behind it, and he could hear sexual pants and moans loud and clear.

"Ahh, you're fucking the shit outta me Suede. Your dick is so big nigga!"

"Take that dick hoe. Take that shit!"

John crept lightly into the spacious bedroom on the balls of his feet unheard. He glanced around the dimly lit room noticing a brown skinned girl sucking on one of her own titties and fingering herself on the couch. Suede was standing up with his back to the door. A female was bent over the bed in front of him, and his hands were tightly grasping her waist as he hit her doggy style. Her legs were spread wide, and her upper body was resting on the bed. Suede smacked her ass with one hand as he rammed himself deeper and deeper inside of her.

John looked on quietly, until the chick getting off on herself came out of her trance and noticed him standing there. He put his index finger to his lips, motioning her to be quiet as he pulled his piece from the back of his pants. She looked on without flinching, her eyes cold and unfeeling. He raised his gun and pointed it towards Suede's back and said, "Now that's what I call getting caught with your pants down nigga!"

Suede jumped backwards momentarily, before attempting to leap towards his pants, which were lying on the floor near the side of the bed. They were out of reach and his movements were too slow. He stood in the middle of the floor naked, his long dick hanging freely. John had already cocked back his hammer, and trained his gun on Suede's head. The girl on the bed frantically grabbed the covers hiding her nakedness, as tears streamed down her face. The freak on the couch still looked on with unfeeling eyes.

"No, no, no, nigga," John said coldly. "Don't make me blast a hole through your fuckin' perm."

"Who the fuck are you nigga? Do you know who you fuckin' wit?"

"With a perm like that, you could only be Little Richard or a punk ass nigga named Suede. So, which faggot are you?"

Suede locked eyes with John, shooting him a menacing glare that was absent of any signs of fear. John cracked a smile in return. He found it noble that he remained brave under the circumstances, but the sight of a buck naked man trying to look tough humored him.

"So, you some kinda tough nigga, huh? You just ready to meet your maker with open arms and shit, right?" John asked. His attention was completely focused on Suede, who smiled slightly as John spoke.

"You done fucked with the wrong nigga here man. I ain't motherfuckin' Woody. I'm a bad man, nigga," Suede boldly proclaimed, as he fearlessly took a step towards John. "Put down your gun, you backwards ass country motherfucker."

John steadied his piece ready to fire, but paused as he saw the light bounce off of the shiny barrel of a gun, off to the left in his peripheral vision. The female who had been pleasuring herself only minutes earlier on the couch, was now standing up pointing a fully loaded piece directly at him.

"Yeah, that bitch there name is Zora. Pretty bitch, huh?" Suede said, as he laughed out loud. "She's fuckin' good as hell in bed, and even better wit a pistol."

Suede wasn't lying. Zora was not only sexy, but equally as deadly. Loyal to nothing but the almighty dollar, she unconsciously killed many men that slept on her because of her stunning good looks. And many a bitch found themselves turned out and hoeing on the track after they befriended her. She was cold and heartless, using the weaknesses of others for her own personal gain.

Sam had crawled out from the bottom shelf of the cart, and quietly made his way to the bedroom door minutes earlier. He hid in the shadows as he heard John and Suede talking. He was tempted to make his presence known, but chose to wait and capitalize off of the element of surprise if the need arose. He was glad that he had waited, when he observed John glance off to his left, obviously in danger.

Sam quietly pulled his pistol out, and gripped it tightly as he peered into the room. From his vantage point, he could barely see the tip of the gun Zora held in her hands. Zora's body was concealed behind the door, which swung inward, and was a little more than halfway opened.

"It's funny how quickly the tables can turn in this motherfuckin' game right?" Suede said smugly.

He had a sly grin on his face. Marie, the girl that was lying on the bed, sat up and pulled her blouse over her head, covering her exposed breasts. A sudden burst of confidence came over her, as she looked towards her female friend and yelled, "Kill that motherfucker Zora!"

John didn't flinch, still standing confidently with his sweaty index finger on the trigger. Suede pointed to his pants, and motioned Marie to retrieve them for him. As she got off of the bed and reached down to retrieve his slacks, a loud blast echoed throughout the suite. Sam had pulled his trigger, sending a bullet exploding through the wooden door. With no line of sight, he estimated where he thought Zora was standing. The bullet whizzed past her face, missing her completely, but effectively catching her off guard.

John seized the moment, as he leapt towards her and delivered a vicious pistol whip to the side of her face. Her body crumpled to the floor, landing in front of the bathroom door. Sam rushed into the room, with his gun trained on Suede. Suede glanced down towards his pants, but seeing Sam and the crazy look in his eyes, made him toss out any notion he had of making a move.

Marie hopped off of the bed when she saw her girlfriend Zora fall to the ground. Hysterically, she ran across the carpeted floor yelling at John, "I'm going to kill you motherfucker!"

In her hand she held a small pocketknife, which she flailed violently through the air, trying to cut John. He jumped backwards to avoid the knife she swung, dodging the brunt of its force, but he still got sliced lightly across his chest. He thought about shooting her, but didn't want to alarm the hotel's guests even further. Instead, he noticed a glass vase on a night table that was within reach. He grabbed the vase with his free hand, and delivered a crushing blow to Marie's head. As she fell to the floor, blood began to flow out of a grotesque gash that the glass from the vase made on her forehead.

Suede held his hands over his head like a fugitive cornered by the police. The confidence that existed moments earlier was now gone.

"What do you motherfuckers want? I got money. A nigga gots money. Just tell me what you want," Suede pleaded.

Sam looked angrily around the room, until his eyes locked onto the two females and he studied their faces closely.

"John, those are the bitches that robbed me. This motherfucker set me up! Let me ice this nigga!" Sam yelled out angrily. His gun hand shook, as he prepared to pull the trigger.

"Wait a minute man. That shit was business. You robbed Black, and we robbed you back. That was business man. Don't make this no personal shit."

Sam lost his temper, and paced towards Suede with his gun aimed towards his head as he said, "You see this scar on my head you fuckin' faggot!"

Observing the madness in his little brother's eyes, John stepped in front of him before he reached Suede. "Relax, baby," John said sternly as he held his hand to Sam's chest. "Let me talk to this yellow nigga for a second before we ice him."

Sam put his gun down angrily, and looked around the room again. He noticed that Zora had regained consciousness, and was sitting up rubbing her head, trying to focus. She licked her lip, which got busted when John pistol-whipped her earlier, before spitting a wad of thick blood that filled her mouth onto the carpet.

"Nah, this shit is personal," Sam spewed coldly, before rushing over to Zora. He grabbed her violently by her hair and dragged her into the bathroom, slamming the door behind them.

"You remember me bitch?" Sam asked coldly. Zora looked into his wild eyes, just as he delivered a backhanded smack across her face, sending bloody saliva sailing through the air. "No? Well I guarantee you ain't never gonna forget me!"

Zora squirmed her body around wildly, defiantly trying to break out of Sam's clutches. She had fought many men who tried to take the pussy when she was growing up, and she just wasn't going to lie down and let him fuck her. She kicked her legs and swung her arms wildly, connecting to his face with a couple of glancing blows. Sam just ignored her punches, and continued to wrestle with her wildly. They rolled on the hard floor for a little while, until he overwhelmed her by pinning her arms down on the cold bathroom tile. He forced his weight on her, grunting as he pried her toned legs open roughly. Anger ran through her veins as she felt him rip her skirt off and penetrate her with his hard dick.

Sweat dripped profusely off of Sam's forehead, as he pushed himself into her loose vagina. She bit down on her lip, and looked off to the corner of the room, still struggling to fight him off in vain. The harder he pounded his penis into her, the more determined she became not to scream. She didn't want to give him any satisfaction.

"So, you like it rough bitch, huh? My dick ain't big enough for you pussy," Sam said, breathing hard as sweat dripped down onto her body.

He turned her over, bending her upper body over the side of the cast iron tub. The cold that she felt against her skin subsided just as a sharp pain exploded in her anus. She let out a loud scream, as Sam rammed his penis into her tight ass. She had never been penetrated anally, and his rough strokes made her rectum feel like it was burning. Tears ran down her face, as Sam gripped her by the waist and continued stroking her harshly.

"You like that, don't you hoe!" Sam yelled out harshly.

Zora was a glutton for pain, who practiced sadomasochism with the hoes and hustlers she fucked with sexually. As he pounded her deeply, the burning in her ass began to become pleasurable for her. She bent over further, arching her back slightly so Sam's dick could penetrate her even deeper. The screams subsided, replaced by erotic moans and pants, driving Sam to fuck her harder. As he continued boning her he reached around her body and pinched one of her nipples hard, causing her to let out an erotic scream. Her pussy began to drip, as he pumped her over and over again.

Zora's screams could be heard clearly in the bedroom where John and Suede stood within a few feet of one another. John tucked his gun in the back of his pants, and told Suede to have a seat. After Suede sat down on the bed, John picked his pants off of the floor and took the gun out of the pocket before tossing the wrinkled slacks on the bed. Suede stepped into his pant's legs, standing up to pull them up around his waist.

The screaming and moans could still be heard from behind the bathroom door. Suede looked over to John with a concerned look on his face and asked, "What the fuck is he doing to her in there?"

"Like I said man, I'm here for business. That shit there is fuckin' personal," John responded.

"Alright…so, what can I do for you? Fuckin' talk to me," Suede said confidently, using his hands as he spoke.

"A nigga named Herbert promised me $50,000 if I take you off of this fuckin' earth."

Suede stood up, and waived his hands in the air animatedly. "Motherfuckin' Herbert put a price on my head! That motherfuckin' faggot! When I see him I'm a kill that fat—"

John cut him short, looking down at the black piece that he held in his hand. "You're not gonna see him again, nigga. When I look at you, all I see is dollar signs, and I intend to cash in. You's as good as dead and I'm as good as paid," John said coldly.

Suede could tell John meant business. Suede was more of a manipulator with the gift of gab, than a killer. But, he had been amongst many. John's eyes looked just as cold as the guys he recruited for his crew. The guys he wished he had with him now.

"There gotta be something we can work out man. I got $25,000 on me now," Suede pleaded.

"If you're worth more dead than you are alive, why should I keep you breathing?"

"Fuck it. I can get you $100,000. I'll give you seventy five fuckin' thousand dollars tomorrow!"

John pondered the thought for a few second, and then he held his hand out. After Suede shook it he said, "You just bought your life back my man."

Suede felt relieved. He had looked death in the eye and was going to live to see another day...another day to get his revenge.

Zora's moans could still be heard from behind the bathroom door. He had never seen that coldhearted bitch do as much as let out a tear. So, he knew that she must be going through some agonizing pain to scream out loud like she was doing. His concerned thoughts for her well being were quickly put aside. Anger burnt through his blood like a wildfire. His mind was focused on Herbert. After a few minutes passed he gathered himself, just in time for an idea to come to mind.

"What's going to prevent you from coming after me again, if Herbert puts more money on my head?" Suede asked in a concerned manner, looking directly at John.

"Good question. I don't know. I mean, I've never tried to murder someone who had me on their payroll. If you catch my drift," John responded.

"So, what are we talking?"

"Five percent."

"Five percent of what?" Suede said exasperated.

"Relax nigga, I'm not a greedy man. Pay me five percent each week of what you make from 129th to 138th, Woody's old turf, which is mostly controlled by me anyway. I don't need to see betting slips or no shit like that. I'll take your word that you're going to treat me fairly. The rest of the shit you make don't concern me. The way I look at it is that no one would be making shit where Woody use to lay his head if it wasn't for me anyway."

After thinking momentarily, Suede said, "I can dig it."

"Hey, listen... if you go after Herbert, I don't want no shit going down between 129th and 138th. I got business over there. I don't want to be caught up in the midst of none of that shit, or have bloodshed on my streets."

"I give you my word that it won't go down by you. But, it's gonna go down."

"Cool. That's on you. Let's just make like this whole shit never even went down," John said.

"Cool. You fucked up my pussy game, and bloodied up my bitches, but I can dig it" Suede responded, cracking a slight grin.

Just then, Sam stumbled out of the bathroom, with his pants undone and hanging low around his waist. He was completely out of breath. Zora's naked body was lying on the cold bathroom floor. She was also breathing heavily. Her pussy was dripping wet from her juices mixed with Sam's semen. She had just gotten raped, but in her own mind, it was the best sex she ever had.

Now standing back inside the bedroom, Sam pulled his pants up, and zipped his zipper before cracking a sick smile. He felt satisfied.

"I took care of my business, did you handle yours?" He asked John smugly.

"Yeah, let's get out of here," John responded.

Suede gave John $25,000 and made arrangements to drop the other seventy-five off at Jive Talk's bar in the morning. John and Sam walked out into the hallway and took the service elevator back down to the main floor. Surprisingly, there was no one in the hallway investigating the source of the ruckus. Petey had been fielding the calls at the front desk over the past half hour, putting the inquiring minds at ease. After the elevator reached the ground floor, they stashed the cart and the uniform jacket back in the break room, before grabbing their coats and quietly exiting back out into the cold.

Curt and Stink sat in the car, with the engine running in order to stay warm. Almost an hour had elapsed, which invoked some degree of concern, but they were immediately at ease once they saw John and Sam walking to the car in one piece. After they hopped into the ride, John told Curt to head over to see Herbert.

Herbert's bar, *The Royal Ballroom* was packed that night. The freaks were out in numbers, and the local hustlers were playing the bar buying drinks. The interior was small. The bar took up one half of the room, and the other half had a dance floor and a handful of small square wooden tables. The overall theme was leopard skin, but the leopard skin carpet, barstools, and tablecloths gave the bar a cheesy feel. Decorating was never Herbert's strongpoint, which was quite evident in the club's interior design and décor.

John walked into the bar by himself, leaving Sam and the rest of his crew reluctantly waiting in the car. He purposely wanted to deliver the money to Herbert alone. And besides, he liked to handle business deals with as few people around as possible. With all being said and done, he also told Sam and Curt to make their presence felt if he wasn't out in a half an hour.

John walked smoothly into the packed lounge, as wandering eyes immediately locked on to him, acknowledging his presence. Herbert was relaxing at one of the tables, with a scantily clad freak sitting on his lap and one of his boys directly across from him. He noticed John immediately when he entered the room, and jumped up excitedly to greet him.

"My man, Johnny Favors!" Herbert yelled out loud. A few members of his crew walked over to greet John. For many of them, it had been the first time they actually saw his face. John slapped each of them five as they introduced themselves to him, before they went about their business. Even after he intermingled with the crowd, John could feel watchful eyes on him as he spoke to Herbert.

"So, what's shaking my man? You want a drink or something?" Herbert asked.

"Nah, I'm alright," John responded.

"You looking good my man. I must say, Harlem's been treating you well," Herbert said as he cracked a smile, and took a sip from the brown liquid in his glass.

John smiled back and said, "I'm doing good, but not as good as you."

"Ha, Ha! Johnny Favors. So, is this visit business or pleasure? It must be business, since my liquor ain't good enough."

"Nah, it ain't like that baby, I just had a long night. You got some place where we can talk in private?"

"Oh, I got you Johnny. Yeah, let's go to my office in the back. It's more quiet back there."

As Herbert led John to his office, he winked at one of his muscular henchmen named Green, who stood discreetly in the corner next to the bar. He finished off his drink and fell in behind them. Herbert sat behind his desk, and told John to grab a seat in one of the leather recliners. As he settled down, Green locked the office door and rested his back firmly against it. John pulled out a knot of bills and placed it on the desk in front of Herbert. He quickly glanced over his shoulder looking at Green, before staring back at Herbert.

"Can I talk in front of him?" John asked in a concerned tone.

Herbert nodded his head and said, "Yeah, he's good. Nothing you say will leave this room."

"Good. Well, I had a little discussion with your man Suede tonight."

Herbert's eyes lit up with the mention of Suede's name. He leaned forward in his seat and asked, "What happened? Is that nigga still alive?"

"Yeah, that nigga was still breathing when I left him. I mean, you didn't ask me to kill him, you just wanted your money back, right?"

Herbert sat back in his seat, realizing that he was acting overly excited. "Yeah, all I wanted was the money," he said, pausing to grab the stash of green off of the desk. "Is this it?"

"Some of it. It's about fifteen g's there."

Herbert sucked his teeth appearing visibly annoyed, as he looked over the knot of money he held in his hand. "That leaves you about ten g's short."

"Nah, baby. It don't leave me about ten g's short. I held up my end of the deal and retrieved your money. That nigga said that he's only giving you fifteen g's. The rest of that shit he said is advanced payment for him to ease up on robbing your spots."

Herbert slammed his hand down on his desk angrily, and stood up. "You hear this shit Green? This motherfucker Suede is trying to extort me!"

Green pounded his fist into his hand and said, "Fuck that nigga Suede, we have to go to war with that nigga!"

John sat back and looked on as Herbert paced back and forth in his small office. He was mumbling curse words under his breath, noticeably disturbed. It was exactly the reaction John had anticipated when he thought of his plan.

"I did that shit as a favor Herb. But, if you go to war with Suede, you can be sure he's going to go at you hard," John said in a solemn tone.

"Fuck him. I'm gonna go at him hard too!"

"Yeah, but you can't be everywhere at once. You're too spread out. You don't even know where that nigga will show up next, or you would've stopped his ass already."

"Well, there must be some purpose to this meeting, besides you telling me that you came up short on my bread."

"Like I said, that shit there was a favor. This ain't my fight, and I'm not trying to get in the middle of this shit. I'm prepared to help you with your problem, but it would be isolated to Woody's old turf. I can guarantee you that none of your spots will be robbed between 129th and 138th going forward. But, it's going to cost you."

Herbert sat down on the corner of his desk, as he thought about what John had just said. After a minute or so passed, his anger subsided and a smile came across his face. "My man Johnny Favors. You always have a plan don't you?"

"I'm just trying to think of something that works for both of us. Understand?"

"Yeah, I understand. I understand clearly. So, what we talking? Five g's a week?"

"Ha, ha, ha....You missed your calling Herb, you should have been a comedian or some shit."

"I had to try, Johnny. *KnowwhatI'msayin?* It's all in good business though."

"Well, let's cut to the chase. I'll keep that nigga off your ass for twenty g's a week. Nothin' more, nothing less."

"Now you sound like the fuckin' comedian Johnny. Where'd you come up with that figure? That's a lot of green."

"Plus five percent of any money you make out of any numbers spots, bootleggers or any other shit you decide to push through Woody's old turf. That's less than you were paying Woody, and probably a lot less green than Suede got from you the last time he robbed you, right?" John asked confidently. He had studied Woody's ledger enough to know that Herbert was dishing out money as well.

"You're not Woody though," Herbert said smugly.

John cracked a sarcastic smile and said, "Exactly. That's why I'm sitting here now."

"You've got a point there Johnny," Herbert said as he stood up from his desk. "I'll give it to you. You've been doing your research, huh? How can you guarantee Suede won't rob any of my spots anymore?"

"That's a good play on words, but I said he won't rob any of your spots in Woody's old area. There's a big fuckin' difference. The rest is on you. And if he does rob one of the spots that Woody used to run, I'll pay you."

Herbert cracked a smile again, even wider than before. "Ha ha, you'll pay me?"

John laughed and confidently repeated, "I'll pay you."

Herbert looked over to Green, who was listening on taking in everything thoroughly.

"You hear this nigga, Green? See, that's what I call confidence. This nigga here is cold as ice. I'm a take you up on that shit Johnny. You drive a hard bargain, but I'm a take you up on that shit. Twenty g's a week and five percent of anything new from 129th to 138th."

John stood up from the recliner and shook Herbert's hand, confirming that their deal was cemented. They chatted it up for a few minutes more, before shaking hands again and parting ways. John's facial expression was unrevealing, not giving away his true feelings. Inside he was elated. In one night, he had deceived two of his biggest rivals, striking deals to generate more cash flow. This shit was a big chess game to him, and his pieces had seized the center of the board. Now, he was strategically planning on taking out the rest of his enemy's pieces one by one. When he got outside and walked to the car, a slight smile came over his face. Things couldn't be looking better for him.

Addiction

CHAPTER 10

Willie sat in a small dusty two bedroom apartment in east Harlem that reeked of old liquor and the stale smell of thick cigarette smoke. The sun peeked slightly through the window, exposing two naked black women in their mid-thirties, laying on a lumpy twin bed in deep sleep. Reggie, an old army buddy he had run into a few weeks back, was out cold on the floor. They had met the two hoes at a bar the night before. Feeling nice off of the liquor, they invited Willie and his friend back to their apartment to continue partying. A few whiskey shots to the head later, they had the freaks stripping and before long they were sexing both of them. Now, a couple of hours later, they lay on the bed half naked and snoring lightly.

Willie was sitting in a shoddy wooden chair that faced the bed, wearing only his boxers, as he stared at the women through wild unfocused eyes. The light glaze that covered his pupils, had been brought on with his high. Now his head bobbed up and down slowly, in a dick sucking motion as his mind floated, completely unaware of what was going on around him.

Reggie and the freaks had shot up first, and then Willie grabbed the needle and shot the liquid heroin into a puffy vein in his ankle. He preferred to use veins that he could keep hidden under his clothes or shoes, but he was running out of good ones to shoot into. As his skinny frame struggled to stay in the chair, a stream of blood slowly ran down his foot onto the floor next to the discarded syringe.

In the dense jungles of Korea, he bravely fought the enemy he had been brainwashed to hate, by the United States government. He viciously delivered death to many *slanty-eyed* gooks, seizing every opportunity he had to take out his anger on them. The hatred that he had for those who killed his father, he aggressively took out on them. The pain he felt for all of the injustice he experienced as a youth, he took out on them.

He hated the racism he had been dealt by the red-necked whites in the south, and now he was using the same anger and prejudice to fuel his disdain for the Koreans he fought. As a result of his bravery, Willie had received several commendations for the valor he exhibited on the battlefield, being recognized as one of the most honorable colored troops.

One evening, as he crept slowly out of the dense jungle into the fields of rice patties, his patrol unit began to take on heavy enemy fire. He barely saw the bright yellow flash from gunfire, before a hot mortar round ripped through the meaty flesh of his thigh, delivering a nearly crippling blow. As he lay on the battlefield grabbing his mangled leg and screaming from the agonizing injury, the medics came to his rescue and injected him with a shot of morphine to relieve the intense pain. His mind slowly drifted off into a state of bliss. This was his first time getting high, but it wouldn't be his last. Like many vets that settled down in Harlem after the war, he had been chasing that high ever since.

"You gotta get up baby. We bout to head out to work," one of the freaks named Lori said, as she nudged Willie, waking him out of his daze. While in the middle of a nod, his eyes regained a slight degree of focus, settling on her face. Dark rings encircled her eyes. He scratched one of his arms uncontrollably for almost a minute straight, before he stood up trying to regain his composure.

"Damn, you's still fucked up, huh baby?" Lori said to him, as she pulled her skirt up to her waist before continuing. "That was some good shit, huh?"

Willie stood up and slowly searched through the scattered debris, clothes and linen that decorated the apartment's floor. Finally, he found his pants and wrinkled shirt. Reggie was still lying on the floor unconscious. Lori had been unsuccessful when she tried to wake him up. Thick saliva dripped from his mouth as he snored loudly, in deep sleep.

As Willie got dressed, he looked at the freak who was still sound asleep on the bed. Lori was trying to wake her up, telling her that they were going to be late for work, but she didn't budge. With no makeup on, Willie couldn't fathom what he even saw in these bitches. But, what he did remember was that the sex was good, and that he got high on their supply.

He stumbled towards the door and opened it up slowly. Lori walked over, still mumbling under her breath, barking at her friend. She had done a good job of hiding the circles around her eyes, creatively using her makeup foundation as she had on several other occasions in the past. Done up, she didn't look half bad. Willie talked to her briefly, before kissing her lightly on the cheek and leaving the apartment.

As he got down to the street, the sun shined brightly into his eyes, causing him to squint awkwardly. He walked aimlessly down the sidewalk, looking for a cab. There were a few other pedestrians on the street, walking about. Everyone who walked past Willie was staring at him suspiciously...or so he thought. As he glared down the street, he saw a uniformed cop walking in his direction. Sweat beads began to form on his forehead, as he nervously pondered his next move. *"Why was the police officer following him?"* He thought to himself, as he suspiciously stared at the white cop that was steadily lessening the distance between them. He contemplated running off...his thoughts were cloudy. As his eyes focused on the sidewalk across the street from him, a car pulled up and stopped right next to him. The car's horn beeped twice, awkwardly catching Willie off guard. He looked at the police officer to his right, and then back towards the car that was now blocking his path across the street, not knowing what to do.

He was about to run, when the car's lightly tinted rear window rolled down slowly, and a deep voice yelled out, "Willie, what the hell are you doing baby?" It was his brother John. "Get in here man."

Relieved, Willie quickly stumbled into the front seat of the car. Stink was driving, and John was sitting in the back seat with Michelle and his son Andre. They had gotten up early to grab some breakfast, and were now on their way to do some shopping.

"What the hell are you doing around here?" John asked, as Stink pulled away from the curb and headed towards 125th street.

"You know, just hanging out?" Willie responded.

"Just hanging out?" John responded in a flabbergasted manner, looking over to Michelle disgustedly. "Man, have you looked at yourself lately?"

Willie looked down at his wrinkled shirt, and awkwardly tucked it into the front of his pants. Then he scratched his left arm as he nervously twitched around uncomfortably in his seat. As Stink continued driving, Willie glanced out of the window. John leaned forward in his seat, and spoke into his brother's ear in a low whisper.

"What's up? Is everything alright with you?" he asked.

John had purposely given Willie his space in the months since they had been reunited. Willie was a decorated army vet, and because of his leg injury, the government was obligated to cut him a check for the rest of his life. Because of this, John felt that there was no need to get him involved in anything illegal. But, Willie didn't look too good.

"I'm fine, man. I'm fine. Give me a damn break John," Willie responded in an annoyed manner.

"You look like shit," John yelled out angrily.

"John, don't—" Michelle said, before John interrupted her.

"Nah, Michelle. I gotta tell my brother the truth. What are you doing, spending all of your money on hoes?"

"Nah, I just been struggling a little lately, that's about it," Willie responded.

Stink pulled the car to the curb, as they approached Ory's on 125th street. After the car came to a full stop, John asked Willie to step outside, so they could talk. Willie was embarrassed that his younger brother was pulling him by the coattails, and putting him in check. But, as he looked back at his reflection in the storefront with a clear head, he saw how bad he looked.

"You're right. I look like shit!" Willie said, acknowledging his bad appearance. Standing next to John, who was sharply dressed in a brand new Italian tailored suit, he looked even more horrible.

"I know I'm right," John said while laughing loudly. "You're my brother, and I ain't never gonna steer you wrong."

Willie sat up on the hood of the car, and looked downward, but in John's direction. "The money they give me ain't enough for me to live on. It's enough to get by, but—"

"You ain't gotta explain to me," John said as he interrupted Willie. "You're my brother. What's mine is yours. You don't even gotta ask."

"But, I don't want no handouts John. I know that you and Skeet got a lot of stuff going on, and I want to be included. I don't just want you to give me money."

"So, you wanna work, huh?"

"Yeah, I want to earn my pay."

"And, what type of work you wanna do soldier boy?" John asked sarcastically.

"Whatever you want me to do, I'm game."

As John embraced his brother, giving him a big hug, a man who had been standing close by for the past couple of minutes looked on. It was Sergeant Glen Charles. Modestly dressed, he would have remained unnoticed, if not for his decision to walk over to John.

"Johnny Favors," Glen said loudly as he approached and stood within arm's length of John.

Stink protectively popped out of the driver's seat when he saw him. But, John quickly held out his hand and motioned him to stay where he was.

"You've got the wrong man. That's not my name," John said as he looked Glen in the eyes. He could tell he was a cop by his appearance.

"No, I think I've got the right guy. And I guess that this is the war hero Willie, correct?" Glen asked confidently. He had been doing his homework for a while, and he knew all the players in Harlem by name.

"Who are you?" John asked coldly.

"I hate when someone answers a question with a question," Glen said, as he took a slow pull from his cigarette. "That shit annoys the hell outta me. But I'm a humor you anyway. My name is Officer Glen Charles."

"I figured you was a pig. What can I help you with?" John asked.

"Well, I just wanted to congratulate you. You know? It's very rare that a poor nigga travels up from the south and does as well as you."

John cracked a smile, as he glanced over at Michelle who was looking on intently from the car's back seat.

"Well, I guess I'm just lucky," John responded.

"Murdering Hayward and Woody without any repercussions—-I'd say that's more than just luck. That's fucking ingenious."

"I don't know what you're talking about," John said, as he paused mid-sentence and motioned Willie over to him.

"Go inside and see if you can find anything you like, while I finish up with Officer Charles here."

Glen smiled sarcastically. He looked inside the car, and waved at Michelle, who waved back politely. Smiling, he turned back towards John and said, "Cute little kid, that's your son, huh?"

"Yeah."

"It's a damn shame."

"What's that?"

"That his father is either gonna end up murdered or in jail. Too many of our boys growing up without their daddies. But, I guess there's no other options for him."

"Nah, his father is a smart business man, he's gonna be alright."

Glen took one last pull from his cigarette, before throwing the butt down on the ground and stomping it out.

"You've been lucky up to this point, but that's about it. You should take your money and run John. Go back down south and buy yourself a farm or some shit. Sell some fuckin' chickens or whatever you country boys do. Cause, if you stay around here, there's only going to be those two options for you."

John smiled slightly and held his hand out. As Glen shook his hand John said, "I appreciate your concern. Mr. Charles, I came up north to avoid the same options that you're telling me I will encounter up here. So, when I weigh the option of returning to the south with racist white motherfuckers, against what you're threatening me with…I guess I might as well take my chances up here."

Glen shrugged his shoulders and said, "Well, good to meet you John. I hope you'll change your mind. In any case, I'm sure we'll be seeing each other again soon."

Glen walked off down the block, disappearing around the corner as John got back into the backseat of his car. Michelle sat quietly, holding Andre who was now sound asleep. She waited a couple of minutes before she asked, "Who was that John?"

"A cop," John responded.

"What did he want?"

"He was just messing with me, that's about it."

Michelle bit down on her lip, before she asked, "Who is Hayward and Woody?"

John looked her in the eyes without flinching and said, "I don't know, Michelle."

"Did you kill them, John?" Michelle asked in a low tone, as her eyes started to well up with tears.

John pulled her closely and wrapped his arm around her, hugging her tightly.

"No, I didn't kill them Michelle. I promise you babe."

She gasped in relief as she asked, "Are you telling me the truth, John?"

"Yes, it's the truth," John said as he kissed her on the forehead lightly.

Just then, Willie returned to the car. He was wearing a sharp new charcoal gray suit, and had four others in a plastic bag draped over his arm. Stink opened the trunk for him, and after Willie placed his items down neatly, both of them sat back inside of the car.

"Did they take care of you, Willie?" John asked.

"Yeah, man. I told them I was your brother, and shiiitt they told me to take whatever I wanted," Willie responded.

John looked over to Michelle. She was staring at him coldly, awaiting his response.

"I spend a lot of money there. I guess they'll get me for the green the next time I stop through."

"Well, any way. Thank you, Johnny. I needed some new suits man. I appreciate it," Willie said ecstatically.

As Stink pulled the car from the curb, Michelle looked out the window. Tears slowly began to run down her face, as they drove past pedestrians and various storefronts. She concealed her sadness from John, by staring out the window the whole trip back to the apartment. Her heart was slowly melting inside of her. As much as she tried to convince herself to the contrary, she knew that she had lost the man she grew to love when he left her to go up north. She was slowly beginning to realize that she barely knew the man she shared a bed with at night.

◆

Suede's stomach lay flat on his king sized mattress, as a sexy latina slowly massaged creamy cocoa butter onto his shoulders. She sensually grinded her bare bikini clad bottom against his lower back as she moaned slightly. The moisture from her wet vagina seeped onto his back, as she moved her round ass back and forth seductively. Suede was on the phone, only half paying attention to her. Black was on the other end of the line, relaying the numbers from the three-five-seven that he had just picked up from the track.

357 was the term they used to refer to the number that came in from the bets placed on the first through third, third through fifth, and fifth through seventh races at the track. By taking the totals from each race, and counting backwards to the third number from the decimal point, they got the three digits that made up the number for the day.

Suede's memory was incredible. When he used to run numbers for Herbert, he always impressed him by being able to sound off all the numbers on the slips he submitted to him off of pure memorization skills alone. But deep down, Suede knew that Herbert couldn't stand him. He was everything that Herbert could never be; smooth, intelligent, and pretty. But, Suede played the game, slowly and methodically manipulating Herbert until he finally got his chance to venture out on his own. Now he used every opportunity he got to shit on Herbert and his operation.

As he visualized the numbers in his head, he recalled that he only had one winner that had played the right numbers in the right order, hitting the number straight. That was a six hundred to one payout, but he wasn't concerned. The cat that played, had only bet twenty five dollars, which left Suede with a fifteen thousand dollar payout to cover. That on top of a few combo payouts, and he calculated about thirty five total he would have to dish out.

He was pulling in more than enough money weekly to cover these minuscule winnings. After making arrangements with Black to pick up the cash needed to cover the bets, he slowly rolled over on the bed. Now he was looking directly in the eyes of the sexy Dominican maid that he hired twice a week to tidy things up around his pad. The hardened brown nipples that highlighted her voluptuous round breasts, looked perky through her sheer white t-shirt.

She smiled at him and seductively asked, "Do you want me to massage your front?"

Suede smiled. Her Spanish accent always turned him on. He put his hand up her shirt, and pinched the nipple on her left breast lightly, before responding, "Yeah, with your mouth."

"Oh, Papi," she moaned while sliding downward and placing her moist lips around his enlarged penis. Suede had his way with her, penetrating her doggy-style and making love to her for about an hour in a few other positions until they both came.

She was his Tuesday and Thursday piece of ass. Spanish with flawless bronze skin and kinky as hell. She was the only freak he let come by twice a week. The other assorted freaks weren't regulars. He'd just call them up when he felt like a piece from a white, black or Chinese whore. Suede had bitches of all nationalities, and he loved to brag about his sexual exploits.

Hours passed, and darkness had began to set in. Suede was now looking through his closet to find some fresh digs to wear to Big Wilt's. The sexy Dominican had been long gone, and he had showered up and was ready to go. After a couple of minutes of deliberating, he decided to go with his cream white Italian suit, and his full-length mink. It was the middle of the winter, but white was never out of season with him. He put a white sky on, with a black brim that matched his black and white shoes flawlessly. Suede wasn't the richest nigga in Harlem, but you couldn't tell by the way he dressed.

Downstairs, Black waited patiently outside of the building. There were three Eldorados' pulled up next to the curb, all bought specifically for this occasion. One for the freaks and the other two for Black and the rest of his killers. When Suede exited the apartment building's lobby, the chauffeur was already waiting with the door held open. Suede stepped inside the car and sat down on the leather seat, after squeezing in between two fine looking hoes. He always rode separately with the freaks.

Everybody who was somebody was out at Big Wilt's that night. Hustlers young and old walked about the spacious club, profiling for the attention of the ever so eager freaks that were standing around dressed to impress.

"Motherfuckin, *Muuuu*-hammed Ali," Suede said enthusiastically as he shook the young boxer's hand. Then he looked towards the bartender and yelled out, "Let me get a round of drinks for the champ and all of his people."

Ali graciously declined, but the rest of his entourage took Suede up on his offer. Even those that weren't with the champ snatched up the free drinks, as the bartender lined them up. Suede loved every minute of it. He didn't get out much, but when he did, he did it right. He was the life of the party.

After things settled down around the bar, he walked across the dance floor with a fine bitch on each of his arms. These weren't any of the hoes that he came with, but two freaks that he picked up within the past twenty minutes. They sat at a table that was off to the side of the dance floor, but in perfect position to observe the entire club. He took a knot of money out of his pocket and spread it out, covering the table in crisp green. Afterwards, he took a sip of his bourbon, before sliding his hand between the legs of the light skinned freak that sat to his left.

Her dimples showed, as she giggled and said, "You're crazy Suede." He smiled back, still playing in her pubic hairs.

As the music played, he continued to take in the environment. Freak after freak tried to find a way to make it over to his table, and he would politely buy them a drink, feel them up, and send them on their way. Girls loved him, and he knew it.

Scanning the dance floor, he noticed a familiar face amongst the crowd by the bar. It was one of those country boys that John sent by to collect money now and then. They never actually met, but he saw him a couple of times. He whispered softly in the ear of the freak that sat to his right, and she walked off in the direction of the bar. Within minutes, her shapely body drifted back across the floor, as she held the hand of a young man who eagerly followed closely behind her. When they made it back to the table, Suede told the young hustler to take a seat. He nervously took the chair next to Suede, and the freak rested her ass squarely in his lap.

"Your name is Stink, right?" Suede asked smoothly, before taking a sip from the brown liquid in his glass.

"Uh...yeah. My name is Larry, but my friends call me Stink. It's a nickname," Stink responded. His voice shook from nervousness, and his southern accent sounded very pronounced.

"My name is Suede. Whatchu drink my man?" He asked.

"Whiskey."

"Damn, whiskey? You didn't look like a whiskey drinker," Suede said laughing, as he paused to tap the freak to his right on the ass. "Go get my man Stink a whiskey, and get me another bourbon."

The girl ran off toward the bar while Suede, Stink and the freak on his lap named Laverne stayed put. Stink wasn't used to getting attention from the ladies. His nickname stayed with him from childhood, a result of constant teasing due to his peculiar smelling breath. Plus, he wasn't too easy on the eyes. So, he was sort of entranced by the fine freak sitting on his lap that was nibbling lightly on his neck.

"That nigga there is about to be the man," Suede said, pointing in Stink's direction, but talking to Laverne. Just then, the girl returned with their drinks and sat back down next to Suede.

Stink took a sip of his whiskey. The liquor quickly rushed to his head, easing his nervousness slightly. Suede told the girls to go off and dance, so he could talk in private. After they walked off, he slid his chair closer to Stink.

"You know, you remind me a lot of myself, right?" Suede said, as he sipped from his drink and looked directly at Stink.

Stink looked down at his suit, and then slowly looked over towards Suede. His own clothing looked like rags in comparison to Suede's digs. Suede chuckled lightly while observing Stink's actions.

"I don't mean the clothes or the shiny ass jewelry, baby. You know, there's only one motherfuckin Suede man," Suede said slyly before continuing. "But, you got a lot of potential, and niggas know that. Trust me. Where you from?"

"South Carolina...Williston to be exact," Stink responded.

"I got family from down there and shit," Suede said enthusiastically.

"Oh yeah, from Williston?" Stink asked in astonishment, being that Williston was a small town.

Suede smiled slightly and said, "Yeah, one of those towns down there. I gots all types of aunts and uncles, running around milking goats."

They both laughed, and continued sipping from their liquor, chatting it up as more and more girls gathered around to get closer to Suede. Stink was enjoying all of the attention.

"I had to come from up under Herbert's funny looking ass, in order to get mines baby. Ya dig? But, you's a cool motherfucker, Stink. Whenever you ready to make that move on your own cat daddy, let me know. I'll help you out," Suede said assuredly.

"Ok," Stink responded, before sipping from his whiskey again. He looked around nervously, not wanting too many people to see him talking to Suede.

"Money never made the man that made the motherfuckin money. You got me? In order to be the motherfuckin man, you gotta make the motherfuckin money that men make. I know I talk fast, but that's only because I refuse to think slow. Ya dig me?" Suede said, pausing to smile and observe Stink's facial expression. "I know. I know. I'm a smooth motherfucker, ain't I Stink? You sitting there saying how can I be that nigga?"

Stink just nodded his head in acknowledgment. Suede read his facial expression, realizing that something was on his mind. He was good at reading people's minds. " I know you probably wondering why a nigga like me would be paying your boss off, right?" Suede said, pausing to crack a sly grin. " Everyone plays a role Stink. You know? I mean I know that I'm not the only nigga paying John. I know he sends you over to pick up green from Herbert too, right?"

Stink nodded his head in acknowledgment again. The liquor was acting as a truth serum. Suede cracked a sinister grin. He played a hunch, and his suspicions were right. He had suspected that John was playing both sides for awhile, but there was no way to confirm it until now. His sinister grin widened.

" But, see that's the way the game is played Stink. And once you understand the game, there ain't shit that can stop you from mastering it. Me and you, we gonna be real cool man. Real motherfuckin' cool, Stink. You's a alright nigga," Suede said slyly, as he patted Stink on the shoulder.

" Yeah, you alright too, Suede," Stink said, sitting back in his seat comfortably. His mind wandered as he took in everything going on around him, not knowing what was right or wrong at that point.

For months he had been running with John, and he never experienced anything like this. John talked the talk, but Suede was living the life that he dreamed about when he was back in the south. The fine bitches, the money and the respect that comes along with it. For a country boy that lived in a dirt-floored shack, with no running water and an outhouse, this was heaven. This was the life he deserved. The destiny he had unrightfully been denied.

At the end of the night, Suede left in the same car he arrived in and headed to a hotel with enough hoes for the rest of his crew. The party was just beginning. Stink slipped out with Laverne, who to his astonishment was still into him even after Suede was no longer around. He took her back to his small one bedroom flat and made love to her over and over for the rest of the night. She was the finest woman he ever had, and he was determined to take full advantage of his newfound popularity.

Hours later, he looked over Laverne's dark sexy skin as the moonlight shined through the blinds in his bedroom, highlighting her curves. He wrapped his arm around her and drifted off into a light sleep. He could get used to this. Suede was right. It was time to get his.

CHAPTER 11

The snow flurries slowly started to sprinkle down on the streets of Harlem a little after four in the afternoon. The radar used by the local weathermen had apparently missed this storm, because none of them made mention of the snow until a few hours before it actually hit. It wasn't a major storm though. Visibility was poor, but it was barely sticking. But as a precaution, the local tracks moved their race times up at the last minute. This was a practice that they often used locally, in an effort to get as many races run before the inclement weather caused the track to be shut down. The only difference today was that nobody saw this storm coming.

John was playing with his son in the living room of his apartment when the phone call came in. Little Andre was running around getting into mischief, while John chased him around like the proud dad that he was. He had spent the entire afternoon hanging out with Michelle and Dre, taking in a matinee movie and doing some shopping before the snow started coming down.

He paused in the middle of a game of hide and seek to pick up the phone just as it rang for the forth time.

"What's happening?" John asked, as he held the receiver to his mouth.

It was Stink on the other end. He sighed slightly before saying, "John, we've got some fuckin' problems man." His voice quivered with emotion, and John could tell it was something serious.

"What's up, Stink? Speak to me," John asked in a concerned manner.

"Shoeless Sam Johnson just called me from the track with the three five seven. The number is 645," Stink said lightly.

"And what's up, Stink? I didn't get the motherfuckin' banking slips from you yet, so what are you telling me?" John asked, his voice now becoming agitated.

"John, three motherfuckers hit tonight."

"Combos?"

"Nah, straights...all three. And they hit big."

"How big is motherfuckin' big?"

"They bet $75, $100, and $200 man."

"What the fuck!" John yelled out loud. Dre started crying , reacting off of his father's emotion.

"Stink, that's $45g's, $65g's and one hundred and motherfuckin' twenty thousand!" John said, multiplying the numbers up quickly in his head.

"And, there's combo hits too John — about ten of those. Big hits also."

"Stink, who the fuck hit the straights?"

"Rell from 125th played the $75. The other two was some new motherfuckers that played with Benny Buds."

"*New motherfuckers?* What the fuck is *new motherfuckers*, Stink? What are you talking about? You sound fucking crazy? What do you mean?"

Stink was growing bitter on the other end of the phone. He didn't feel that he had done anything to deserve this type of treatment. He bit down on his lip and shook his head before saying, "John, I don't know what you're talking about...I—"

John interrupted him yelling loudly, "That's your fuckin' problem Stink, you don't fuckin' know shit! This amount of motherfuckers don't fuckin' hit all at once, just out the blue. And, this is *new motherfuckers? New motherfuckers?* Where the fuck are you now, Stink?"

Stink was taken aback. He paused before responding, "I'm...I'm on 116th street."

"Stay the fuck where you are. I'll be right there," John said before slamming down the phone. He grabbed his jacket and car keys off of the dining room table. Michelle came out of the bedroom and grabbed Dre, who was still crying uncontrollably. She rubbed his back lightly, calming him down as she walked over to John with a concerned look on her face.

"What's wrong John? Why were you yelling like that? What's going on?" Michelle pleaded.

John kissed her on the forehead, and turned to walk out the door just as the phone rang again. Agitated, he walked briskly over to the set and snatched the receiver off of the switch hook.

"Didn't I tell you I'd be right over there motherfuc—"

"John! John!" Sam yelled, interrupting him mid-sentence. "John, it's...it's Willie. He overdosed."

"He what? What happened, Sam?" John asked, as his heart dropped to the pit of his stomach at the sound of more disturbing news.

Sam sobbed before saying, "I found him in his apartment with some bitches John. He had a fuckin' needle dangling from his arm."

"Is he dead, Sam? Is he dead?" John asked.

"No, we're at the hospital. But, he's in a coma, John. They said it was heroin. He overdosed on fuckin' heroin." Sam mumbled, his words drifting off.

"Heroin? Willie overdosed on heroin. I can't believe this shit. What hospital are you at?'

"Harlem. John, I did everything I could do. He wasn't moving. I tried to pick him up and get him to walk, but he was barely moving. I didn't know what to do...I — "

"Sam, you did good. Don't blame yourself. You did all you could do. I'm on my way," John said, consoling his younger brother, who was sobbing on the other end of the line.

"O.K, I'll be here," Sam said, as he hung up the phone.

John hung the receiver up hesitantly, before walking over to Michelle and hugging her tightly. His eyes were withdrawn, and his facial expression unfeeling. By now, Dre had cried himself to sleep. His head rested on her shoulder. Michelle had gotten the gist of the conversation by listening to John's responses. She hugged him with her free hand, and asked in a low whisper, "Is he going to be alright?"

"I don't know, Michelle. I just don't know," John said as he sobbed and shook his head from side to side. He couldn't even ponder the thought of losing his brother. He had just returned to his life after being gone for so many years.

"When it rains it fuckin' pours."

With that he kissed her on the forehead and said, "I love you," before walking to the apartment's front door.

As he opened the door and walked into the hallway, he said "I'll call you from the hospital." Michelle nodded her head in acknowledgment, as tears flowed down her face uncontrollably.

John rushed over to the hospital, driving as quickly as humanly possible. He struggled to focus his thoughts. His brother was on his deathbed, and his business was coming apart at the seams. He felt like he was losing control.

Sam was waiting outside the hospital lobby, smoking a cigarette when John arrived. It was his third in the past twenty minutes. His nerves were on pins and needles. As John hugged him, he observed his bloodshot eyes. Sam was visibly shaken. Willie's overdose had obviously taken its toll on him.

"How's he doing Skeet?" John asked in a concerned tone.

"He's in a coma, but they got him stabilized," Sam responded.

John looked him in the eyes and said, "Is he going to make it?"

"They don't know. But, they say he's doing better than when I checked him in," Sam said, as he paused to take a pull from his cigarette. "If they can keep him stable, they'll move him out of ICU and we'll be able to go up and see him."

"How long has he been doing this shit? I mean, who was he with?" John asked.

"Some bitches I think he met the other night. They were high as fuck too. I couldn't get much out of them though. From what I hear though, there's a lot of GI's coming back from the war strung out and shit," Sam responded quietly.

John changed the subject asking, "Did you hear about all the people that hit today?"

"No. I been dealing with this shit. How many?" Sam asked inquisitively.

John lowered his voice when he spoke, noticing the amount of people walking in and out of the hospital. "Three motherfuckers hit, fuckin straights."

"Three? What the fuck?"

"Three. And two of these motherfuckers played at Benny's. They hit big Skeet."

"How big?"

"I can't cover this shit. They won big."

The hospital's front door swung open, and a black doctor wearing a white lab coat with a stethoscope draped around his neck stepped out. Earlier, he had promised Sam that he would come down and give him an update when they had some news to report. Willie was still unconscious, but they were pretty certain that he would pull through. It was a definite overdose. After the doctor gave them a few more details, he let them go upstairs and take a quick peek in on him.

Willie was lying face up in the only bed in his small hospital room. He was no longer hooked up to a respirator, he was now able to breathe on his own. John and Sam looked over his body concerned. He looked like he was lifeless. Both of their eyes had a watery glaze about them. An IV was slowly feeding him fluids and medication through a tube that was inserted into a vein in his arm. They didn't speak to one another as they looked at their older brother. Sam still blamed himself, convinced that he could have done more...that he should have been with his brother.

John looked at Willie and immediately thought of the day that they saw their father get brutally murdered by racist white men down south. Willie had never been the same since. When they followed their father's orders, running off and leaving him behind to face his certain death, a piece of Willie died as well. From that day on, John never ran away from anything again. Willie on the other hand, never stopped running. As John stared at him, he realized that his brother was still trying to escape his past. Instead of running off to the army, he was now using drugs to escape reality.

As their thoughts wandered, five minutes quickly turned into fifteen. Even though he wanted to give them more time, the young doctor that granted them time to see their brother, had to ask them to leave so the hospital staff could perform more tests.

Once John and Sam reached the lobby they agreed to go their separate ways and meet back up at John's apartment in an hour. John still had to go see Stink. In the meantime, he told Sam to start heading over to their number spots to see how much money they took in today. He was trying to pool together as much money as possible. It was a thought. But even still, he knew he would come up way short on what he owed.

As they walked outside, they noticed a peculiar looking dark colored sedan that idled silently in front of the hospital. Their instincts told them that something was wrong. Sam tucked his hand in his jacket pocket and gripped the cold handle of his piece tightly. With all of the mayhem, John had rushed out of his apartment forgetting to pack his .45. Now he felt completely naked as he sat in front of the hospital, staring at the suspicious looking car. He tucked his hand in his pocket, pretending to grip a gun.

As they stood by the hospital's door, the seconds that immediately followed passed slowly. After a couple of uneasy minutes, the rear passenger's side door opened slowly, and a middle-aged Italian man walked out.

It was Luciano DelBracio. Dressed in a dark gray Italian double-breasted suit. He looked like the typical mafia henchman. Luci walked over to John and extended his hand before saying, "Johnny Favors?" His Italian accent was deep and well pronounced. John took his hand out of his pocket and shook his hand firmly.

"Luciano DelBracio," Luci said, as he continued gripping John's hand with his pudgy fingers. "But, my friends call me Luci."

After wrestling his hand from Luci's grip, John said, "How can I help you?"

Sam looked on suspiciously, standing close by, still gripping his piece tightly.

"We need to talk...in private," Luci said. Snow flurries had began to come down heavily, and people hurriedly walked into the hospital's lobby. Luci looked around. His facial expression showed his uneasiness with talking in public. Sam looked over to John, who nodded his head letting him know everything was ok.

"Let's talk," John said, before following Luci back over to the sedan. Luci opened the back door, and slid across the spacious backseat of the Lincoln. As John stepped into the car, he looked back at Sam.

His facial expression exuded confidence, putting Sam somewhat at ease. When the car door closed, the driver pulled off quickly from the curb unexpectedly. John became slightly nervous, but he didn't let it show outwardly.

"So, Johnny we finally get a chance to meet," Luci said, cracking a smile as he glared at John. John's facial expression never changed as he stared into the man's eyes.

"I've been patiently waiting to meet the man that's been costing me one hundred thousand dollars a week."

"Let's cut the small talk. Money is time, and I don't like to waste time or motherfuckin' money," John said smugly.

Luci stared at him, still cracking a slight grin. "I think I've heard that somewhere before. But in any event, from what I hear, you've recently inherited a huge debt, and you're gonna need a lot of time to come up with the money that you owe. And time is definitely not on your side, by the look of things," Luci said, laughing slightly under his breath.

John didn't respond, his facial expression remained cold as he looked squarely into Luci's eyes. Unfazed, Luci pulled a cigar out of his suit pocket, then he fumbled around his pocket a little longer until he pulled out a silver lighter. Before lighting the cigar, he glanced up at John and cracked a sarcastic smile again before saying, "I know there's a lot on your mind with your brother laid up and all."

The comment caught John's attention. The Italian obviously knew more about him than he

196 ONCE UPON A TIME IN HARLEM

imagined. Their encounter definitely wasn't just by mere coincidence.

"So, you've done your homework, huh? That's cool, but my family is personal. If you've got business to discuss with me, speak. If not, you can drop me back the fuck off."

"Ha,ha,ha,ha...I like this guy, Louie," Luci said, laughing as he tapped the back of the driver's seat. Louie, his chauffeur laughed out loud as well.

"So, what do you want to talk about?" John asked impatiently.

"I have a proposition for you," Luci said, pausing to light his cigar. "You need money. Don't let foolish pride or an overgrown ego cause you to lose sight of that fact. I've seen it happen a thousand times."

"What's your proposition?" John asked inquisitively, loosening up a bit.

"I've got five hundred thousand dollars for you. That should more than take care of your outstanding debt," Luci said.

"And what do you want from me?" John asked curiously.

"It's simple. We helped Woody establish his network in Harlem, and together we controlled the uptown numbers racket for years. You came along and killed him. No harm, no foul. Business is business, and the numbers game is numbered. The fuckin' government wants their piece of the pie. They're the motherfuckin' biggest crooks around. You know what I'm saying? They're fuckin' cocksuckers," Luci said emphatically.

He had John's complete attention now. He looked on attentively and asked, "So, what do you want from me?"

"The network is more important than the numbers. Heroin is the next big thing. Your clientele is already established, and you already have the storefronts and nightspots to use for distribution. It would be easy as hell for you to make the transition. I'll front you the money to pay off your debts, and once you pay me back, we can work as partners. It's a fuckin' no brainer."

John's thoughts wandered momentarily, as he began to think about his brother Willie. A few hours earlier, he had overdosed, and now he was considering a proposition that would have him peddling the same lethal substance that almost killed his brother, to others. His conscious didn't necessarily agree with it, but he couldn't rule it out, because he didn't know any other means of getting the money to pay off his debts.

He was usually good at making decisions on the fly, but he couldn't fully convince himself as to what action to take. Hesitantly he said, "I have to think about it. It sounds good, but I need to think it over."

"I understand, it's a big move. A chance to make some real money, and a real name for yourself," Luci said, pausing to take another puff from his cigar. "But, as you said — time is money. I don't expect to wait around long for an answer."

"I can dig it. I'll have an answer for you tomorrow," John said assuredly.

"Sounds good. I'll wait for your call. Here's my number ," Luci said, as he scrawled a telephone number on a small piece of paper and handed it to John.

They made small talk for a few minutes, while the driver navigated through the streets of Harlem,

returning John to the hospital where they had
initially picked him up. As the sedan pulled up to
the curb, Sam walked over, greeting John as he exited
the car. His concern turned to elation when he saw
his brother.

"Is everything ok?" Sam asked, looking past
John momentarily towards the car behind him.

"Yeah. How's Willie? Any updates?" John
asked.

"The doctor just came down. He said that
Willie opened his eyes for a quick flash. They want
him to get some more rest before he has visitors,"
Sam said.

"That's good," John responded excitedly.

"So, who was that?" Sam asked.

"Mafia," John said.

"The Italians? What the fuck did they want?"
Sam asked.

"It's a long story. Let's go grab a bite to eat
and talk about it," John responded.

◆

The evening meeting at Harlem's mosque
number 113 ran over its scheduled time, due to an
unexpected visit from the Islamic Nation's leader.
Most of the Muslim contingency gathered inside felt
blessed by just being in his company, but one
individual in the audience mind was elsewhere.

After the customary prayer, and the standard
"All praise is due to Allah," the meeting ended and
the crowd slowly began to disperse. Paul
Weatherspoon, or brother Paul X, the name his
Muslim brothers knew him by, moveed quickly

through the crowd towards the exit. He had an important meeting to attend. One that would change his life drastically.

As he exited the mosque, he made a left and walked quickly towards the closest corner. After walking swiftly down the block, he made a right onto an intersecting street. He looked around nervously, until he saw the dark sedan parked at the far end of the block. Still continuing at a brisk pace, he walked across the icy pavement that coated the street, and made it to the car in no time. He was so focused on making his meeting that he didn't even hear the young voice calling his name behind him.

Maurice Rivers was a young teenager that idolized Paul. Paul was one of the nation's trusted security officers, and the respect he garnered was unquestionable. So, when Maurice saw Paul hurriedly run out of the mosque leaving his Koran in his chair, he retrieved it and quickly followed behind him. But, Paul was moving too swiftly for him to catch up. He yelled his name out aloud, but with the chaos and noise in the air, his words only carried a few feet.

Maurice didn't know why Paul would be in such a rush. He usually stayed behind to assure that everyone safely made it out of the mosque. That was one of his responsibilities. Breathing heavily, he made it within a few feet of the car that Paul had disappeared into, as it pulled away from the curb. Peering through the foggy window of the sedan, he caught a glimpse of the driver as the car sped away. As he struggled to catch his breath, he wondered why Paul would be speeding off down the block with a pig.

In the car, Paul began to feel a little more at ease. He had never met Glen so close to the mosque before. They had been meeting at the diner across town for almost a year now. He had covered his tracks carefully, and was certain that no one had followed him. It was risky, but it was a risk that was worth taking. This meeting couldn't wait.

As they drove, and put some distance between them and the mosque, Glen eased up off of the gas pedal and pulled his car to the curb. Weatherspoon had contacted him earlier, and refused to talk over the phone. This was the first time they had an impromptu meeting, so he knew that it was important. He lit a cigarette and looked over at his passenger.

"So, what's on your mind Paul," Glen asked, before taking a pull from his cancer stick.

Paul's eyes lit up excitedly. "You have to promise me that this is it. This shit is over after this. I get my life back—you, you have to promise me," Paul blurted out emotionally.

"I need to know what you got for me before I agree to anything," Glen responded coolly, hiding his excitement.

"I got what you want. Just give me your word that this is it."

Glen nodded his head in acknowledgement. "If you've got what I want then you've got my word. This is it."

Paul let out a sigh of relief as he dug into his coat pocket. He was sick of living a lie—sick of the deceit. He just wanted to get this over with so he could have his life back. After a few seconds of digging around in his pocket, he pulled out a folded white envelope and handed it to Glen.

"What's this?" Glen asked inquisitively.

Excitedly Paul responded, "Open it up."

Glen unsealed the envelope and pulled out a thick wad of rubber band wrapped cash. It was ten thousand dollars to be exact. He stared at it for a couple of minutes in silence, before he shifted his attention back to Paul, who was sitting back in his chair with a slight grin on his face.

"I can't be bought Paul. Your debt to society means a lot more to me than a few thousand dollars," Glen said angrily.

Paul sat up in his seat defensively as he said, "I'm not trying to pay you off."

"Then what is this Paul?"

"Do you know who John Williams is?"

Glen's eyes lit up as he said, "Yeah, the two bit hood they call Johnny Favors. Yeah, I know him, why?"

"That's his money."

"How did you get it?"

"He gave it to me. Or rather, he gave it to Bilal and he gave it to me to put away."

Glen's complete attention was captured now. He threw his cigarette out the window, and looked Paul in his eyes excitedly.

"What does he give Bilal money for?"

"To fund different activities and events that we have around the community. I mean, it's never been communicated to us directly, but in turn, we know not to hassle any of his people on the street."

"The Muslims are being funded by murderers and number runners," Glen whispered lightly under his breath. A light bulb went on in his head that brought a smile across his face. This was it. He had

202 ONCE UPON A TIME IN HARLEM

followed his hunch, and it turned out to be right. He always knew that there was a criminal element involved with the Muslim movement, but he couldn't find an angle. Now he had one, and with solid planning, he could take down two criminal organizations at once. His seat on the City Council was all but guaranteed.

"How often does Williams give him money?" Glen asked inquisitively.

"Every Sunday. He gave me this earlier today, and he'll be dropping off another ten g's next week," Paul said confidently.

A huge smile came over Glen's face, as he patted Paul on the shoulder. "You've done good son...you've done real good. You just tell me when and where the drop off is, and I'll be there next Sunday. After that, you can have your life back."

Paul thanked Glen. He was ecstatic. The last year of his life had been a living nightmare, and in seven days he would be able to put it all behind him. He gladly gave Glen the information he needed. He couldn't wait to get this whole ordeal over with.

At the same time across town, Benny Buds was closing up his small corner store, that also served as an after hours liquor and numbers spot. Benny was a middle-aged family man that now ran with John, but previously he rolled with Woody when he was in his prime and Bumpy before that. Harlem had its fair share of drunkards and winos that were always looking for a bootleg after hours spot to get their spirits. Benny stayed open late on Sundays specifically for that purpose.

As he took a stack of greenbacks out of the cash register, and placed it in his pocket, a look of satisfaction came over his face. His time was well spent. Business had been good for him tonight. He had gotten a call from an Italian connect of his at the track earlier in the evening, that tipped him off to the fact that the races had come in early. They sent two brothers over to play the winning numbers straight, and then he passed the slips off to Stink. The night had indeed been a good one, but tomorrow would be even better once he collected his percent of the earnings.

He closed up shop and cautiously walked to his car. One hand was in his pocket gripping a black piece, and the other clutching his car keys. Some young punks had robbed him about six months back and he no longer took any chances. As he walked, the moonlight illuminated the street, allowing a clear line of sight to his car. After unlocking his car door, he sat in the driver's seat and let out a sigh of relief as he pressed down the lock.

Benny started the car, and was just about to place it in drive, as two gloved hands clutching a thick metal wire slipped around his neck. Benny was usually very observant, but he didn't notice that the interior light was out in his car when he unlocked the door, and he also failed to see Curt's frame hidden in the back seat.

Excruciating pain shot through his body, as the pressure being applied to the wire caused its exposed metal threads to rip through the muscles in his neck. The cold shiver of fear ran through his entire body. He screamed in agony, before the thread ripped into his windpipe, causing his cries to turn into inaudible gasps. His arms flailed wildly in the air, and his legs kicked erratically, smashing the windshield and causing the horn to sound loudly several times. He continued to struggle valiantly, to no avail. As blood sprayed out of his neck, soaking the tan interior, death swiftly began to set in. The struggle was over as quickly as it started. His body went limp, and crumpled in the front seat.

Curt slowly and methodically wrapped the bloody wire up and placed it in his jacket pocket, while looking outside through the window of the car to make certain that there were no witnesses. After confirming that there was no one around, he sat Benny's body up in the seat, by grabbing a handful of his thick afro and using his other hand to pull him up by his blood drenched shirt.

As Benny's lifeless body sat propped up in the car seat, with his head dangling downwards, Curt methodically pulled two pieces of paper out of his pants pocket. He reached around the seat and shoved both of them into Benny's mouth, before he calmly got out of the car and walked down the street disappearing into the night.

When the police found Benny's body later that morning, the first thing they noticed were the two peculiar looking pieces of paper shoved in his mouth. Upon removal, they discovered that the bloodstained crumpled pieces of paper were actually numbers slips. Both of them were identical. They had the numbers 645 written on them, a couple of initials, and the word "straight" scribbled in blue ink.

CHAPTER 12

John spent the entire morning at the hospital, sitting at his brother's bedside. Willie was not only conscious, but he was also eating on his own. The doctors wanted to keep him hospitalized for a few more days, out of concern for his health. They had warned John, that the next couple of days would be the hardest on his brother. Heroin was a highly addictive drug that resulted in a habit that was severely difficult to quit. The young doctor that treated Willie had an aunt that succumbed to a heroin overdose. So, he was very compassionate about treating its addiction. He promised John that he would do whatever he could to help his brother's recovery.

John was very grateful. He loved his brother Willie. His heart crumbled just seeing him like this. Apparently, Willie had become a pretty heavy heroin user that needed a hit often. His checks were all being spent to support his high, and the cold sweats and hallucinations that he was now experiencing, were clear evidence that his withdrawal was going to be a rough one.

Earlier that morning, John and Sam had a long discussion about the Italian's offer. John was skeptical. They wanted him to peddle a drug that had his older brother throwing up and going into convulsive fits. It didn't sit well with his conscious. But, Sam was a little more optimistic. He coldly thought about the money that could be made, due to the addictiveness of the drug. He knew that there were already apartments in Harlem used solely for people to get high. If they could control its distribution, they could control Harlem.

John knew he was right about its addictiveness and money making potential. Even though it didn't sit well with his conscious, he didn't really have much of a choice. He didn't have the money to cover his debts. He had gambled and lost. If he went to one of his rivals for a loan, it would expose weakness. They would pounce on him in a heartbeat. The Italians had him where they wanted him, and they knew it. John had called them an hour ago and set up a meeting for tonight. He would get the money he so desperately needed, and in return they would become partners distributing heroin through his number's network.

John was a little concerned about how the other local hustlers would react to him entering into the heroin game. Suede refused to pay Stink last week when he sent him to collect his regular weekly pick up. He also wasn't returning any of John's calls. John figured that he probably found out he was getting played. Herbert on the other hand, was still holding up to his end of the bargain. He was a little weird, but ultimately, John realized that he was harmless and reliable.

John couldn't afford to go to war with both of them at once, so he decided to make an offer to Herbert. With both of their networks being utilized, the influx of money would only increase. Besides, Herbert was easily influenced, and John knew that he wouldn't have to worry about being challenged by him. Suede, on the other hand still had a chip on his shoulder from their run at the hotel. He had something to prove. Herbert was definitely the better choice. He would deal with Suede later if need be.

After spending a few hours at the hospital, John and Sam headed over to *The Royal Ballroom* to have a sit down. John had called Herbert earlier, and stressed the importance of having a meeting of the minds. Herbert was a little suspicious at first, but he quickly agreed. He could hear the urgency in John's voice, and he was curious to hear what he wanted to talk about.

John and Sam arrived at Herbert's spot around one in the afternoon. The main room with the bar was virtually empty with the exception of two of Herbert's henchmen. Sam grabbed a bottle of gin from behind the bar, and poured himself a double shot. He chose to stay put and shoot the breeze with Herbert's boys, while John handled his business in the back. Sam was fatigued and stressed out. The hot shot immediately hit the spot.

Herbert was sitting behind his desk, puffing a fat cigar when John walked into his office. Sitting in a chair in the corner, slightly hidden in the dim light, was a man that John never saw before. He quickly got up and extended his hand warmly. It was Leroy Gates.

John shook his hand politely, as Leroy said, "Johnny Favors. I've heard a lot about you."

John cracked a slight smile and responded, "Don't listen to anything that Herbert had to say, he lies a lot ya know."

Leroy laughed and said, "No, I'm inclined to believe what I've heard about you. My name is Leroy Gates. It's a pleasure to meet you."

"Same here," John responded, as he took a seat in one of the chairs facing Herbert's desk. Leroy sat back in the corner, and began reading a legal case journal while John and Herbert spoke.

Their conversation was very brief, considering the seriousness of the matter. John explained to Herbert how the Italians had approached him, their proposition and the role that he would like Herbert to play in the whole scheme of things. He left out the part about him needing cash to cover outstanding debts. Herbert listened intently, his facial expression and demeanor seemingly unmoved. After John explained everything, he asked, "So, the Guineas want to get back into Harlem, and they approached you, huh?"

"Yeah, basically," John responded.

"And, the fuckin' I—talians suggested that you work out a deal with me?" Herbert asked, before taking a slow pull from his cigar.

"No, fuck the Italians. I wanted to include you in on this shit. I think this is a perfect opportunity for both of us, that's why I reached out to you," John said firmly.

Herbert smiled sarcastically. He glanced over to Leroy, before looking at John and saying, "So, you're looking out for me?"

"It's a business proposition. But, it's up to you. I'm a make this green regardless, ya dig?" John said confidently.

Herbert smiled and laughed loudly, slamming his hand on his desk. "Here you are doing me a favor again. You alright with me Johnny. This nigga here is alright!" Herbert laughed out loud again, his stomach vibrating under his shirt. John and Leroy laughed as well, caught up in the moment.

After the laughter subsided, John got back to business and asked, "So, are you interested?"

Herbert smiled and said, "Hell yeah, I'm interested Johnny. We got a deal. We just need to work out the numbers."

"Cool. I have to meet with the Italians tonight, and we'll sit down tomorrow and work out the details," John said as he stood up and shook Herbert's hand. Before John left, Leroy walked over to him and shook his hand, closing the office door behind him. Herbert sat behind his desk and pulled from his cigar, as Leroy sat in one of the chairs in front of the desk.

"So, whatcha think?" Herbert asked, looking directly at Leroy.

"I think it's a good opportunity," Leroy said.

"Fuck that Leroy, the Italians should be dealing with me directly. Fuck this middle man shit!" Herbert said angrily, his demeanor changing considerably.

"Herb, you gotta be smart about this shit. The Italians may not have come to you directly, but they'll know that you're involved. Before long, you'll have your own connect."

Herbert frowned up his face. He was fuming inside. The Italians passed him over to deal with John, just as they had passed him over to fuck with Woody. That shit pissed him off to no end. Leroy knew Herbert well. Without any words being spoken, he could read his facial expression and tell what he was thinking.

"Herb, trust me. Your time will come. You just have to be patient," Leroy said calmly.

"But, I should be — "

Leroy interrupted him and said, "And you will be."

Herbert nodded in acknowledgment, "You're right. You're always fuckin right. I won't do nothin' stupid. You're fuckin' right."

◆

After the sun set, the only visable light was provided by the moon and old streetlights that were erected on each corner of the narrow blocks that zigzagged through the Little Italy section of Manhattan. Mulberry Street was lined from end to end with new cars, mostly Lincolns and big bodied Caddies. Many popular Italian hangouts and restaurants were located on this block, traditionally known for its Mafioso ties.

Luciano DelBracio had dropped four suitcases off at *Veliz*, the stylish home style Italian restaurant that he used to launder dirty money, and conduct meetings with other made men. He never liked being around to actually participate in any handoffs. Jimmy Two Tone, the restaurant's manager usually orchestrated any deals that needed to take place. Jimmy got his nickname from the pink birthmark that awkwardly stretched across one half of his face.

The four suitcases were stored in a storeroom, next to flour, yeast, and other supplies used daily to make the fine fresh bread that the restaurant was famous for. Three of the suitcases were packed to the hilt with the finest grade heroin manufactured in opium factories in Mexico. The forth suitcase was filled with thousands of untraceable large bills, tightly packed in compact bundles.

The whole plan was rather simple, as Luci explained to Jimmy Two Tones. Two niggers would be arriving at eight in the evening. They would enter in through the front of the restaurant, head directly into the rear of the restaurant, and grab the suitcases out of the storeroom by the back door. Then they would exit out the back and onto Mott Street. This wasn't the normal modus operandi, but Luci didn't want any niggers hanging around longer than necessary. It was better for everyone involved, if they got the spooks in and out.

A quarter after eight, Stink pulled in front of *Veliz*, in a black Lincoln. John and Sam slowly hopped out of the back and walked towards the restaurant, while Curt stayed put in the shotgun position. By the time John and Sam entered the restaurant, Stink was halfway down the block, headed towards the pickup spot on Mott Street. He purposely drove slowly knowing he had a few minutes to kill. It wouldn't be cool if two black guys were sitting in a car idling at the end of an alley in Little Italy, for more than a few minutes. And also, he didn't want to draw any unnecessary attention.

The restaurant was only half full when John and Sam walked into the lobby and scanned its spacious interior. The tables were aligned close to one another, with three rows neatly juxtaposed. They made minimal eye contact with the restaurant's patrons, as they headed towards a door with a sign above it that read, "STAFF ONLY." Slipping virtually unnoticed through the door, they were surprised to be greeted in the kitchen by Jimmy Two Tones.

"Hey, what's up guys?" Jimmy asked in his normal gruff tone. The kitchen was abuzz with chefs and helpers preparing Italian cuisine with traditional herbs and spices. The workers ignored John and Sam's presence. The heat from the stoves and ovens made the climate quite uncomfortable. Sweat was beaming off of Jimmy's forehead. He shook both of their hands quickly before saying, "Follow me."

They navigated through the workers that frantically scrambled around, carrying plates and saucers full of tasty delights. Finally, they reached the storeroom located in the back of the restaurant. John immediately saw the four medium sized suitcases on the floor.

"That's it?" John asked, looking Jimmy Two Tones in the eyes.

"Yeah, that's it bro," Jimmy responded.

Jimmy quickly popped open each suitcase and showed them the contents. He asked John if he wanted to count the money, knowing that he would decline the offer. He had the Guineas heroin and their money. There was no reason for him to fear being cheated. After securing the clasp at the top of each suitcase, Jimmy handed two suitcases a piece to John and Sam, before leading them to the back door.

"Mott Street is to your left," Jimmy said as he held the door open for them. They nodded their heads in acknowledgment, before walking past Jimmy and exiting into the dark alleyway. A cold uneasy feeling came over John as they stepped outside, but he quickly shook it off, regaining focus.

Rats scurried through the foul smelling garbage that spilled out of two dumpsters that were pressed up against the brick wall on opposite sides of the alleyway. The moonlight peeked through the darkness providing minimal illumination as they walked towards the end of the alley that led to Mott Street.

They both walked at a brisk pace until they reached Mott Street. As their eyes adjusted to the light provided by the street lamps, they scanned the block until they noticed Stink down the block and off to their left. He drove up the street slowly as he saw John and Sam walk out of the darkness.

John held the suitcases tightly in his hands, as he waited patiently for Stink to drive up. Cold air blew across his face, a reminder that the bitterness of winter was still present. Out of nowhere the silence and serenity was interrupted by a sound that resembled a car backfiring. Sam jumped nervously when the sound echoed through the block. John felt uneasy. His eyes scanned the block slowly, as he studied the cars on the street. He didn't see anything that seized his attention. They both glanced at each other, before continuing timidly down the street. The look of concern was in both of their eyes.

"BOOM!" Another loud sound echoed throughout the street, piercing the silence that existed only seconds before. John noticed a slight movement in the shadows behind a car parked off to his right. He tried to focus in on the shadowy figure. But, before he could react, a hot slug ripped violently through his right shoulder. The .45 caliber bullet exploded out of his back, sending small chunks of flesh and bloody mist flying out into the cold air. The impact of the bullet spun his body ninety degrees, sending one of the suitcases sliding across the pavement, as he fell backwards to the ground.

Sam dropped to the ground, taking cover behind a blue Cadillac as a bullet whizzed over his head, barely missing him. He grabbed his .38 out of his waistband, aimlessly shooting bullets into the darkness. After a few seconds passed, he glanced over to his brother, not realizing that he had been shot. John was sprawled out on the ground, slowly creeping towards a space in between two cars on the street, in an attempt to reach a safe haven. Bullets collided with the pavement around him.

As the sounds of gunshots echoed in the air, Curt hopped out of the passenger's side door clutching a sawed off shotgun. He spotted one of the killers cautiously walking towards John's direction. Without hesitation, he squeezed down on his trigger before the killer was able to train his pistol on him, yelling *"WhatamIawoodorwhat,"* as his slugs ripped through the man's chest plate.

His victim crumpled to the ground with a loud thug and an anguishing scream. Instinctively, Curt felt a presence behind him. A slight chill came over his body as he started to turn around, but his reaction time was too slow. It was as if he was moving in slow motion. He heard the sound of the two bullets exploding out of the killer's cannon. But, he barely felt the hot slugs as they blasted through the back of his head, sending brain matter the size of watermelon chunks onto the concrete.

Curt's lifeless body fell to ground, just as the sound of shrieking tires reverberated through the narrow street. It was the sound of Stink speeding off down the block. As he made his getaway, he failed to negotiate the turn off of Mott Street at a slow enough pace. He pressed down on the brakes too late, causing the car to slide into a parked sedan. Stink's head slammed forcefully into the windshield, shattering it on impact. The force of the collision knocked him into an unconscious state.

Still hiding between two parked cars, John heard the loud crash of the accident at the end of the block. Sharp pain shot through the left side of his body, as he fished through his jacket pocket with his right hand, until he located his piece. Lying on the ground, he was able to see the feet of one of the killers as he cautiously walked in his direction. He leveled his pistol, pointing it under the trunk of the car, and sent two bullets whistling through the air. One missed. The other bullet hit its target, ripping through the hit man's ankle, severely crippling him.

As the man stumbled to the ground, Sam crept into the street and shot him twice in the chest at point blank range. Blood streamed out of his body, onto the paved street. Sam observantly looked around him. After being sure that no other killers were hiding in the shadows, he glanced back at the man he had just shot. His face was familiar. It was Link Johnson, the killer that he had a run in with at the pool hall ages ago. He knew that Link was a hired gun, but he wondered who had put up the fee for his hefty price tag.

By now, John was on his feet. Agonizing pain still shot through his body. He nursed his bloody left arm, as he came to his brother's side, completely consumed with anger. He had a suitcase in his right hand, which he placed down on the street before grunting, "Go get the motherfuckin' car, Skeet. I'll gather up the money and the Her-on."

As Sam ran towards the car, John dropped the suitcase and pulled out his piece. He looked at Curt's lifeless body. Driven by anger, he turned towards Link, and emptied his piece into the front of his head. His face exploded into an unrecognizable mush, as the five bullets delivered at close range tore his skull apart.

Sam jumped when he heard the sound of gunfire echo behind him. He looked back at John, before continuing to run down the block at full speed, stopping once he reached the site of the accident. The driver's door was open, and Stink was still sitting behind the wheel, with his body facing towards the street. He was holding his bloody forehead in his hands.

The car was still running. Surprisingly, it only had minimal damage with the exception of the shattered window, and the hood and bumper being pushed back on the right side. A couple of bystanders had gathered around, but they quickly walked off when they saw a black man run up brandishing a piece.

"Stink, what the fuck did you drive off for? They shot John!" Sam asked, as he reached the car.

Stink glanced up at him, barely able to focus, still feeling faint from the head trauma he had just suffered. His brain and his lips were not working in unison. He babbled without thinking.

"I didn't know this was gonna happen. He didn't tell me he was gonna do this shit…I'm sorry Sam," Stink said as his voice drifted off into an inaudible whisper.

Sam looked at him in disbelief. He had no idea what his childhood friend was talking about.

"Who the fuck is he, Stink? What the fuck are you talking about?" Sam yelled out.

"Suede. I told him. I said that the Italians were going to meet with you and John and—"

Hot anger shot through Sam's veins as he yanked Stink out of the driver's seat of the car, and threw him forcefully onto the concrete. Placing his gun flush against the side of his head, he shot him twice. Then he coldly kicked his lifeless body over, before he sat in the car and threw it in reverse.

The steel bumper rubbed slightly against the front tire, causing slight friction and a rubbing noise, but it was more of an annoyance than anything. Sam was able to drive the car in reverse down the block, pulling up next to John who was kneeling down holding what was left of Curt's head up.

Sam jumped out of the car, grabbed a couple of suitcases and threw them in the trunk. As he put the second set of suitcases in the trunk he said, "Get the fuck up Curt, we gotta get outta here. John, tell that nigga to stop being a bitch."

Tears were in John's eyes. He looked down at Curt, no longer feeling the pain from his own wound. "He's dead Sam. They fuckin' killed him," John yelled out in an agonizing cry.

Sam rushed around the car and looked down at his friend in disbelief. He opened the back door of the car, and after struggling for a minute or so, he was able to hoist Curt's body up and into the backseat.

"Come on, we gotta get him to the hospital. They can help him. They'll be able to save him John," Sam muttered. His words betraying his true feelings. Deep down, he knew his friend was already dead.

John jumped in the passenger's seat and they sped off down the street. By now, more onlookers had nosily wandered outside. Looking over at his brother John asked, "What happened with Stink?"

A look of disgust came over Sam's face. "It was that nigga Suede...that motherfucker Suede set this up."

John sat up in his seat, giving Sam his complete attention. "He said that Suede set us up?"

"That nigga was mumbling some shit about Suede. Talking about he's sorry and some shit. He didn't have to come out and admit it, he said enough. I sent two bullets through his head and read his fuckin' mind," Sam spewed out coldly.

John looked at his friend's lifeless body in he backseat, and cursed under his breath. He wondered how things had spiraled out of control so quickly. He blamed himself for not being more cautious, for not planning this shit out better. He couldn't bring Curt back to life. But, he sure as hell planned on bringing the motherfucker responsible to a slow and painful death.

When they were a safe distance from Mott Street, Sam slowed to the speed of the cars around him. Police cruisers sped past them, headed at a feverish pace towards the murder scene. When they reached Canal Street, John told Sam to pull over. He was bleeding profusely. He felt lightheaded as his body slipped into a cold shiver.

Reluctantly Sam pulled over and said, "I gotta get you to the hospital, John." He feared that his brother was going to go into shock.

"No. Call Bilal. He'll have someone that can help us. We can't go to the fuckin' hospital. The fuckin' pigs will be on us like white on rice," John muttered weakly, his words sounding shaky as they left his lips.

"Ok, I'll be right back," Sam said as he jumped out the car and walked past an elderly Chinese couple as he made way to a nearby payphone. He called Bilal at home, waking him up out of his sleep. After explaining the situation, Bilal told him to go see a doctor named Hezekiah Jones, with a private practice located in Brooklyn. He was right across the Manhattan Bridge, and it would be quicker for them than if they headed back to Harlem. He told Sam to head over there now, and he would meet them within an hour. He had some things on his mind that he needed to speak to them both about anyway.

Sam hung up the phone and placed one more call before heading back to the car. He sat down and grabbed the steering wheel with both of his hands that were sticky from dried blood, and sped away from the curb. John was applying pressure to his wound with his right hand, attempting to slow the flow of blood.

"Don't worry John, I'm a take care of you...and the motherfucker responsible for this shit," Sam said as he headed towards the Manhattan Bridge.

Back in Harlem, Suede was sitting on the king-sized bed in his apartment, resting his back against the headboard as he smoked a cigarette. Zora was dancing on the carpeted floor in front of his bed, getting off on herself as she felt on her body seductively through her scantily clad dress. She had surprised him by popping up about fifteen minutes ago. He hadn't fucked her in a few months, and he didn't have any of his other bitches coming over tonight, so he was happy to see her.

After her striptease act, she got down on her knees slowly. She put her index finger in her mouth, using it to simulate a sexual act, before calling Suede over to her. He got out of the bed and pulled off his boxer shorts, his dick hanging half way down his thigh as he walked over to her.

When he reached her, she kissed the head of his penis lightly and used her hands to massage it softly. Suede closed his eyes as she flicked her tongue on the tip of his penis, sending chills through his spine. He moaned lightly, feeling her warm saliva on his tip. As his manhood got harder, Zora used her tongue to extract a razor blade she had hidden on the base of her mouth. This was a trick she had mastered as a youngster, during a stint she spent in a home for delinquent teenagers.

Securing the razor's blade tightly between her lips, she clutched his penis in his hand, and quickly jerked her head downward. The razor ripped halfway through Suede's erect penis. Before he could react, Zora used her left hand to pull a small knife out of her garter belt, quickly stabbing him in his lower back puncturing his kidney.

Suede screamed loudly as he clutched his penis with one hand, and his lower back with the other. His eyes were stricken with confusion and fear, as he stared at Zora in disbelief. Blood poured out of his body quickly, emptying onto his carpeted floor. As he fell to his knees, Zora backed away from him slowly. She grabbed her high-heeled shoes from off the floor, and rifled through one of the night table drawers until she came across about ten thousand in cash.

Suede was lying on the floor, begging for help in ghastly whispers. His pain brought her pleasure. His suffering made her feel serene. As she walked past him headed towards the apartment's door she softly mumbled, "Business, never personal, nigga."

CHAPTER 13

Sam dished out some major green, sparing no expense to organize a homecoming party for his older brother John at the *Maltese Ballroom*. It was Saturday night, and over a hundred hustlers, hoes and close friends piled into the ritzy establishment adorned with crystal chandeliers, beautiful Italian rugs and expensive oil paintings that hung from marble walls connected to high cathedral ceilings.

Little Frankie Lymon the crooner, graced the crowd by hitting a few high notes from his various hits, between sets by the hired band. It was indeed a stellar event. For one night, under the same roof, the likes of Bilal and his Muslim contingent intermingled with street hustlers like Herbert. They had all gathered to show support for a man that they all affectionately called, Johnny Favors.

The party started at ten o'clock, but John, Sam, and Willie didn't walk through the door until a quarter after twelve. Exiting a chauffeured Rolls Royce, the three of them stepped out draped in matching full-length minks that rested right above their ankles and black and white pinstripe suits. John's arm was in a white sling, but other than that, he looked good as hell as he walked into the ballroom flanked by Sam and Willie.

This was John's coming out party. He tossed his normally modest get up, for a crisp thousand dollar suit and an expensive gold diamond studded pinky ring. The flower pinned under his left collar was looking crisp and smelling fresh. A week ago he had looked death directly in its evil eye and cheated it. Now he decided it was time to live a little.

"Johnny Favors. My main man. You're lookin' good," Herbert said enthusiastically, as he hugged John tightly. He was the first to approach him when he arrived. He had been to John's apartment twice during the past week, expressing his concern.

"Hey Herb. Sam told me that you stopped by. I appreciate that man," John said sincerely.

Herbert smiled, exposing his yellow teeth, as he hugged him again. He tried to maintain a conversation with John, but a crowd had quickly gathered around them, vying for John and Sam's attention. Before long, Herbert was an after thought as John entertained and shot the breeze with the hordes of people that approached him.

There were so many people in the joint, and all of them were dressed to kill. Willie had already drifted off to the bar with a scantily dressed young lady that seemed very eager to make his acquaintance. He had gone more than a week without a drink, and was eager to wet his whistle. His body yearned for the feeling that he felt when he shot up, but he tried to contain the urge by dousing himself with the taste of alcohol. He grabbed a stool by the bar, in between two fine looking freaks and made himself comfortable. He was in his element.

Sam made the rounds, chatting it up with the hustlers and flirting with the freaks. As he took in his environment, a fine stallion wearing a skintight dress approached him and kissed him lightly on the cheek.

"Hey, baby," she whispered softly in his ear, as she smiled seductively. "I've been missing you." It was Zora. He hadn't seen her since the night she killed that nigga Suede for him. Five thousand dollars and some long stiff dick was all she charged him to take Suede off of this earth. It was well worth it. He kissed her on her lips, before saying, "I'm a stop by later." Satisfied, she smiled as she walked off, disappearing into the thick crowd of people.

Liquor was flowing freely, reducing everyone's awareness and their inhibitions. In the bathroom stalls, street niggas smoked reefer and had sex with whores that swallowed their manhood's whole. The atmosphere was completely carefree.

Bilal chose the right moment to stroll over and introduce John to a young protégée of his named Maurice, who he recently added to his security detail. John greeted him enthusiastically, striking up a brief conversation before they headed out. He knew that this wasn't your typical event that would be attended by Muslims, and he appreciated the fact that they had made the effort to stop by and see him, even if they only stayed for a hot minute.

As John walked through the crowd, an older Jewish gentleman named Sal approached and introduced himself. A jeweler by trade, Sal explained to John that there were some ways that they could make each other rich. John didn't know much about jewels and rare stones, but he told Sal that he would arrange a meeting in the next week. He was interested to hear what he wanted to discuss. The prospect intrigued him.

Fine women were hanging on John like a cheap suit, as he showboated, enjoying every minute of it. Everyone knew that he was the man who took Woody out and also that he had his hand in a big part of Harlem's numbers game. They all wanted to be around him. The aura was enticing. He was the center of attention.

Herbert sat at the bar drinking bourbon straight. The liquor rushed to his head making him feel nicer by the minute. Music was blasting and the dim lights made him feel as if he was in a hypnotic state. It wasn't that long ago, when everyone wanted to be around him — when he had to beat the hoes off of his arms when he went out on the town. Now everybody and their mother was gathering around John. It was as if he didn't even exist.

Still staring at the ballroom floor, he observed the crowd through drunken eyes. His lawyer, Leroy Gates was involved in a deep conversation with John. They were sitting at a table across the room with a few other people, talking it up and laughing uncontrollably. Fuming inside, Herbert stumbled off of his barstool and walked over to them, rudely interrupting their conversation.

"Well, well, well. I see that you're even paying homage to the king of Harlem, huh Leroy?" Herbert said in a drunken slur.

Embarrassed, Leroy politely said, "Excuse him, John. He's had a little too much to drink."

"*Excuse me*? I don't need no goddamn excuse. I'm just having a good time. This is a party ain't it?"

Herbert blurted out loudly, getting the attention of those close by. He struggled to maintain his balance, as he stood in front of John.

"Yeah, it's cool Gates. Everyone is having a good time. No need to fuck up my man Herbert's high," John said.

"Man, I remember when this motherfucker was broke as hell, beggin' fo work and shit," Herbert said as he leaned closer to John. "Funny how things change and shit, right?"

"Yeah, life is unpredictable like that," John responded calmly.

"Yeah, I'd fuckin' say so. Everybody give it up for the king of Harlem," Herbert yelled out as he held his glass in the air, imitating a mock toast. A couple of people close by actually toasted him as he stood in the middle of the crowd. Leroy looked on embarrassed, before putting his arm around Herbert and attempting to lead him away from John. By now, a lot of people were looking on at the spectacle taking place in the middle of the ballroom.

Herbert pushed Leroy's arm off of his shoulder forcefully and said, "I'm sorry John. I'm sorry, man. This is your night. Can't nobody take that away from you. Woody couldn't take this away from you. Shiiitt. Motherfuckin' Link Johnson couldn't even take this shit away from you."

John bit down on his lip, as anger rushed through him. He stood up from the table, but quickly gathered himself and scanned the crowd with his eyes before saying, "You got the wrong nigga, Herb. It's your world, baby. I'm just the man standing next to the man."

Herbert smiled and hugged John tightly as he said, "I love you, John. I fuckin' love you."

John hugged him back, whispering in his ear, "It's ok, Herb. It's ok. Love fuckin' hurts sometimes. I forgive you though, nigga. I fuckin' forgive you."

As Leroy led Herbert off, John looked at those around him and sarcastically said, "That's the reason I don't drink too much. Alcohol ain't no damn good for you. That shit'll kill you."

The crowd that was gathered around laughed aloud hysterically. The mood quickly changed and John continued partying on into the wee hours of the morning with his brothers unfazed. This was the first time that he fully realized how powerful he had become and the impact that he had on other people. The feeling was addictive, but it was also scary as well. Now all eyes were on him.

The next morning Sergeant Glen Charles awoke before the crack of dawn. The butterflies that gave his stomach an uneasy feeling, had kept him up all night. But, he didn't need sleep. He was still functioning off of the pure rush of adrenaline. Three days ago, his commander had approved a requisition for the small task force that he needed. He was even given the authority to handpick his choice of officers from a short list of seasoned black officers that were highly respected.

He had done a superb job of documenting his findings and communicating the details of his investigation to his commanding officer. It was a hard sell, but Glen had put his career on the line to get the approval he needed. He successfully sold his boss on the press that the department would garner from this high profile bust. Glen was on top of the world.

Twelve plainclothes officers were positioned at various locations in and around *Rubie's Diner*, blending into their surroundings seamlessly. After speaking to Weatherspoon last night, Glen had put the final touches on his plan to take down the Black Muslims and John's gang in one clean sweep.

It was a quarter after nine, and the diner was beginning to fill up. Weatherspoon was already fifteen minutes late, but Glen wasn't overly concerned. Looking out the window of his sedan, he waited patiently. As he stared through the sun's glaring rays, he looked on as Bilal arrived flanked by a bodyguard and a young man he hadn't seen before. His confidence suffered a minor blow, but he tried to shake it off. He had expected Weatherspoon to accompany Bilal, but for some reason he was missing in action.

Ten minutes passed before a shiny blue Lincoln pulled up in front of the diner. The driver stayed in the car, keeping the engine running, as the passenger stepped out of the car and walked briskly into the diner. One of his hands were suspiciously tucked into the deep pocket of his black leather trench coat. Glen watched on intently. He had seen the car before. It belonged to John's crew.

Weatherspoon was still a no show, and the window of opportunity was closing quickly. Thoughts raced through Glen's mind, before he made a split second decision. He already had two of his men inside of the diner. He glanced at a young officer named Dave that was set up across the street at a payphone outside of the diner, and gave him a hand signal. After signaling back, Dave put the phone on the hook and walked slowly into *Rubie's*.

The inside of the diner was bustling, as the waitresses hustled to service the patrons that filled each table, as quickly as humanly possible. There were parents accompanied by their young children dressed in their Sunday best, patiently waiting to be served. Dave blended in with the people standing just inside the entranceway waiting to be seated. In the midst of all of the chaos, he spotted the shady looking man that had just walked into the establishment standing in the back room next to Bilal's table.

A brief discussion took place, before the man looked around suspiciously and handed a thick folded envelope to Bilal. As soon as the exchange was completed, two plainclothes officers seated right outside of the room jumped up from the table revealing pistols that they had been concealing.

"Freeze motherfucker, hands up!!!" One of the officers yelled. Breakfast dishes flew off the table and shattered as they hit the floor, alarming the other patrons in the diner. With speed and precision, the officers quickly ran into the room as Dave secured the dining area by waving his gun in the air.

The man that gave Bilal the envelope only seconds earlier, tried to bolt from the room when he noticed the cops. But, one of the officers pistol-whipped him across his forehead violently, dropping him to the floor with a loud thud. The other officer grabbed Bilal by the collar and threw him on the floor as well. He pressed his knee into the middle of his back, as he placed metal handcuffs around his wrists tightly. Bilal screamed out in agony as the officer cracked a sinister grin and said, "Listen to your leader crying. Where's Allah now bitch!"

Bilal squirmed angrily, but quickly realized that he was struggling in vain. With his face pressed against the ceramic floor he asked, "What is going on here? What are you doing?"

"You know what's going on. Where's the envelope, motherfucker?" The officer said angrily.

"In my pocket. It's in my jacket pocket," Bilal yelled out.

The muscular officer's adrenaline was rushing as he reached into Bilal's pocket and pulled out the folded envelope. He didn't even notice the flashes from the cameras that were going off around him. He was too focused. He ripped open the thick envelope and held it up in the air.

"What are you doing?" Bilal asked the officer again, but he ignored him. By now the deflated officer had examined the booty he recovered from the envelope. Dumbfounded, the officer looked around in disbelief just as Sergeant Glen Charles had strolled into the back room.

Reading the expression on the young officer's face, he asked, "Where's the envelope? How much money did they pay him?"

The officer passed the envelope to Glen hesitantly. To his astonishment, it was only filled with a thick wad of raffle tickets. A hot flash came over him as his heart dropped to the pit of his stomach. A couple of camera flashes went off again and he angrily tried to find the culprit, but the crowd was beginning to grow unruly.

With their tails between their legs, Glen and his team took the handcuffs off of Bilal and walked out of *Rubie's*, as the rowdy crowd threw plates of food and glasses at them. A small riot ensued as the group of Muslim's agitation began to grow. As the officers drove off down the street, the word, "Pigs" reverberated through the air. Glen had gambled and lost. The operation was a complete failure. The local news stations had been tipped off, and the stationhouse was buzzing with calls from concerned citizens and government officials by the time Glen and his team returned. The Muslims had done an excellent job of distributing their pictures and telling their story to the local media. The department was receiving a tremendous amount of heat.

After a brief interrogation, Glen was placed on a paid leave. He would find out a few hours later, that a couple of officers performing a routine sweep of an abandoned building had uncovered the lifeless body of his informant. Weatherspoon was the apparent victim of a heroin overdose.

What Glen didn't know is that the last meeting he had with Weatherspoon had bought him his death sentence. A young ambitious Muslim named Maurice had seen Weatherspoon get into Glen's car, and tipped Bilal off that fateful night. Glen was oblivious to these fine details, but he smelled a rat and his name was Johnny Favors. In his mind, John had single-handedly shattered his dreams of gaining a seat on the city council.

He sat on a lumpy mattress in his messy bedroom and took a swig from a brown bag that concealed a bottle of Jack Daniels. As the spirits rushed to his head, he made a silent vow to himself. He promised that he would bring down John and his crew, even if it took him the rest of his career.

♦

Herbert walked into *The Main Event*, a small men's clothing store on Broadway, with his right hand man Green. He had on his favorite olive green blazer and black slacks. Herbert was still nursing a slight hangover from the night before, but two aspirins and a hot cup of coffee had helped him brush off most of the ill effects. He browsed the clothing racks, looking for just the right blazer to fit his sense of style.

Even though Herbert didn't coordinate his clothing well, he always spent a pretty penny on his wardrobe. The rack that he was sifting though had jackets that cost three hundred dollars and better. Most of them were loud vibrant colors that were already out on the racks in preparation for the upcoming months of spring.

Green was trying on an expensive European tailored suit in the fitting room, while Herbert continued to browse through the rack with his back to the door. He didn't notice the young disheveled looking black male that walked into the store and politely greeted a sales girl that welcomed him at the door.

Methodically, the man slipped behind Herbert and without hesitation pulled out a black piece that had been hidden in his waistband, before sending two slugs whistling through the back of his head. The sales girl screamed, as blood and brain matter splattered onto the expensive suits. Herbert's heavy frame collapsed forward onto a rack of clothes, hitting the floor with a thud.

Green burst out of the dressing room just as the gunman was calmly strolling towards the front door. The killer heard the disturbance behind him, and tried to quickly duck behind a clothing rack. As he went for his gun, Green sent a bullet blasting through the side of his neck, shattering the store's front display window. The patrons and the store's employees ran for dear life, screaming loudly. The killer stumbled backwards, returning fire before he collapsed to the floor from his grave wound.

Outside a car sped off and Green ran over to Herbert, whose body was sprawled out across the floor. Green frantically lifted him up from the suits that were already saturated with his dark red blood and held him in his arms. Sensing that he wasn't breathing, he attempted to perform mouth to mouth, to no avail.

Herbert's body shook violently, as his strength departed from his body. For once, he had gone against Leroy's advice, and attempted to have John murdered. And then, he let his liquor get the best of him at the party last night. Not even the police knew that the body of the black man they had uncovered on Mott Street, with his face splattered across the alley, was Link Johnson. Alcohol is truth serum, and what he said had cost him his life.

Herbert's bloodshot eyes rolled back in his head. Brain matter oozed onto Green's lap as he held his mushy skull, and said a silent prayer to himself. His boss was dead.

The rooms in John's apartment were strewn with cardboard boxes filled with clothes and various other items that were neatly packed away. John and Michelle had settled on an elegant four bedroom brownstone in Strivers Row, that they would be moving into in the next couple of days. They had grown out of space in their current pad, and besides, he wanted something a little more fancy for them.

John sat at his worktable, with Dre propped up on his lap. He had grown considerably since his second birthday a few weeks back, and now he was rambling off words from his growing vocabulary list.

John's left arm was still healing, but he used his right hand to meticulously carve a sculpture out of a block of wood he had clamped securely on his worktable.

He skillfully used his knife to carve out the facial features, using the craftsmanship that he had learned from his father, when he himself was just a boy. He had learned well. And even with him using his only free hand, he was able to work magic. Dre watched on intently as his father worked with the soft wood. John's thoughts drifted as he reminisced about the past.

His father only wanted a chance at the American dream, but instead he encountered the American nightmare, as so many blacks from the south had. John would have suffered the same fate, had it not been for several unforeseen events. Holding his son close to face, he looked deeply into his eyes. He resembled Sam when he was younger, and this scared John. What had he become…what would his son become?

He had just sold his soul to the Italians, agreeing to a pact that had pulled him deeper into the underworld. He didn't want this for himself or for his family. His life and the fruits of his devious deeds had become as addictive as the drugs that Willie had succumbed to, and he didn't like it.

Michelle walked into the room quietly and sat in a chair next to John. She loved to see him like this, playing the fatherly role with Dre. It was times like this that made her believe that buried somewhere deep inside of John, were remnants of the young man that she fell in love with.

John looked up at her, coming out of deep thought. He noticed that she had a glow upon her face. This caused him to smile and put his carving knife down on the table before saying, "What is it?"

Michelle smiled embarrassingly, then her eyes dropped down into her lap and she replied, "Nothing, it's nothing."

"I know it's something. I can see it all over your face," John said.

Michelle smiled again, still looking downwards. After a few seconds passed, she looked up and said, "I'm pregnant John."

John's face lit up, as he jumped out of his seat in excitement. He placed Dre on the floor and hugged Michelle with his free hand.

"I knew it, I knew it!" John yelled out in elation.

"No, you didn't," Michelle said as she hugged him back tightly.

"Yes, I did. Yes, I did," John said loudly, just as the phone rang. He kissed Michelle on her forehead, and released his tight grip on her, before walking into the living room and answering the phone.

"Hello," John said as he held the receiver to his ear.

The voice on the other end hesitated before saying, "It's done. We got that nigga about a half an hour ago. Harlem is yours now. This whole fuckin' city is yours, Johnny."

John hung the phone up on the switch hook, and walked back in the room with Michelle and Dre. He took her back into his arms, kissing her sensually, hiding his true feelings.

This moment was symbolic. He had just learned that he had a child on the way, the same time his enemy was murdered. Death spawns life. Herbert's death had paved the way for new opportunities. Now, there was definitely no way out.

Once
upon a time
in
Harlem

BOOK ONE

written by:

Moses
Miller

About The Author:

Moses Miller is an author, journalist and co-founder of Mind Candy, LLC, a company focused on book publishing and creative screenplay development. A native New Yorker, Moses exhibits the uncanny ability to capture the pulse of the streets with intelligence, strong character development and well thought out storylines. Moses has contributed articles and written for various websites and publications including The Voice, Newsday, 88HIPHOP.com and F.E.D.S. Magazine. He holds a Bachelors degree in Business Management and a Masters of Science degree in Technology Management. His first novel, Nan: The Trifling Times of Nathan Jones has received critical acclaim from critics, readers and book clubs around the world.

For book club meetings, speaking engagements or to provide feedback directly to the author please email:

info@MindCandyMedia.com

Also Available From Moses Miller...

NAN:
THE TRIFLING TIMES OF NATHAN JONES

ISBN: 0-9786929-0-X

"When I was thirteen, my parents were killed in front of my eyes. Ironically, I would spend the rest of my teenage years being raised in an orphanage with another individual whose parents were murdered by the same man--on the same night. Before I turned twenty, I would be at war with a corrupt NYPD unit...and live to tell my own story."

Nathan "Nan" Jones